"Do you find me attractive?" she said.

I was ready to choke. Be honest, I told myself. "I must confess, I've never seen a woman as beautiful as you are. I find you exquisite. Everything about you—your hands, your face, the way you walk, the way you smell—I know this sounds horribly crass, but I find myself thinking of making love to you." God, what had I done? I was just being honest, I told myself, but Geeez, did I have to put myself in jail? I guess I'd better get ready to leave—no way was I getting this job. No way was I coming back here at all. I was too ashamed to look at her, so I looked out the window. I should get up now. I said to her, "It's probably time I left. I don't think I should be here...." And then her hand was on my arm and I turned around to face her.

She looked at me for what seemed like a week, and then she said: "Make love to me, then. I want to feel what it's like to be made love to by a woman."

Tools of the Trade

K. T. BUTLER

ROSEBUD

Tools of the Trade
Copyright © 1996 by K.T. Butler
All Rights Reserved
An electronic version of this title was
originally published by Spectrum Press.

First Rosebud Edition 1996

First Printing March 1996

ISBN 1-56333-420-8

Cover Photograph © 1996 by Michele Serchuk

Cover Design by Dayna Navaro

Manufactured in the United States of America
Published by Masquerade Books, Inc.
801 Second Avenue
New York, N.Y. 10017

Tools of the Trade

The Best Summer of My Life

"Come on, Johnny, hurry it up. Ain't got all day," I whined. He was so slow. "You are slower than molasses in January," I declared, and Gregory made that little high-pitched giggle he was so fond of. "You sure do talk funny," he said. "And so do you, pisgetti-head," I said as we shuffled off through Johnny's back yard. Gregory couldn't say "spaghetti"—he pronounced it "pisgetti." Being from Virginia, I was a stranger in an even stranger land of Pennsylvania. All the other kids made fun of my drawl. Not Johnny or Gregory. They just attributed my speech to the fact that I was different.

I was different. Even my father said so. I hardly ever saw him because of his business trips. One time he and my mom were standing in the kitchen. I was sitting at the kitchen table reading. I learned to read the newspaper when I was three and I haven't put it down yet. I was engrossed in the paper but I managed to hear Daddy say, "but she's different." And I knew he was talking about me. How different I didn't quite know. But it was the summer of 1962 and I was about to find out.

So I was whining at Johnny to hurry it up. The Three Amigos—Johnny, Gregory and me—were off on another adventure and I didn't want to waste time. The summer days were gloriously long and filled with bright, blinding sunshine. Who knows what awaited us? We could run down to the creek and try to catch minnows, which I found incredibly boring. I saw no benefit whatsoever in sitting down quietly and trying to snare lousy little fish that you couldn't even eat! Now crabbing, that was a fishing activity that had some benefit. Back in Virginia we used to go crabbing on the Potomac, before it got so polluted. But I wasn't in Virginia anymore. I had to make do with minnows.

"Let's go 'round the block, then to the park. And maybe later we'll scare some girls," Gregory said. Although Gregory was the youngest of us at four years old, he was clearly the leader. Later on, my therapist would say that I allowed him to dominate me, even to the point of letting him talk me into doing things I knew I would get in trouble for later. But I was six years old. Thoughts of Gregory's dominance becoming a pattern for me later in life were not even a blip on my mental horizon. Scaring girls, this was a great idea.

Somehow, the fact that I was a girl did nothing to dissuade Gregory and Johnny from including me as one of the boys. According to them, I was really a boy. I was just missing a piece. Gregory always said that my mother must have been in such a hurry to have me born that they pulled me out of the line when God was handing out dicks and that's why I didn't have one. "But you're a boy, just like us. You act like one and think like one. Maybe you can get one later." Whatever Gregory said, I tended to believe him. His explanation seemed logical enough. I was a very intelligent child, but when it came to common sense, my mother said I didn't have any. Maybe I got pulled out of that line too.

Whenever I watched the other girls playing with their dolls and frilly things, I thanked God every day that he almost made me a boy. It seemed stupid to devote energy to dolls. They were incapable of conversation, incapable of movement. Nothing like a nice frog or a turtle. The girls didn't have any clue, did they? And they must have known that I was an almost-boy because on the few occasions I did play with them, they always made me the daddy when we played house.

I modeled myself after Dr. Alex Stone from The Donna Reed Show. I was infatuated with Donna Reed. I would pretend that Carol Shibelli was Donna Reed as I gave Mommy a kiss. I really liked that part. Sometimes I would pretend I hadn't gotten it right and could we have do-overs, please, and then I'd get to kiss her again. It was not the first clue, but one of the strongest clues I would have about who I really was.

We climbed the fence in Johnny's back yard, ran through the tangles of weeds and overgrown brush and ran down the hill until we were into "the park." The park wasn't really a park like the parks of today, with benches and flowers and stuff. It was just a large, open area of land that the creek ran through. But there was something else outstanding about the park—the storm sewer! This incredibly huge concrete tunnel with water running through it. We used to go inside the sewer and follow it for what seemed like miles. Actually, we managed to go from Sixteenth Avenue to Fourteenth Avenue—a mere two blocks. We thought we were world explorers.

It was never more exciting than when we were halfway to Fourteenth Avenue and this big rush of water came through. We clung to the sides and watched the stream gush past us. I prayed that we wouldn't see any rats. I knew rats had to live in a place like this, and secretly I wished we would turn around and go back. If Gregory and Johnny had an inkling of my thoughts, they'd know for sure that I wasn't a real boy, so I put on my brave face and announced that we should continue on toward Fourteenth Avenue. At Fourteenth Avenue, there was a grilled manhole cover and we could actually see the cars passing over us. We would sit on the rocks and Johnny would pull a copy of Playboy from his knapsack and we would ooh and ah at the pictures. I liked the cartoons, though I didn't know what any of them meant. As I was the only one who could read (Johnny was five and a bit slow, his parents said), I would read the descriptions underneath the pictures of the naked ladies while Gregory and Johnny talked about how big their tits were.

Today we decided on a quick tour of the sewer, then a dip in the creek. "But how're we gonna scare the girls?" Johnny wanted to know.

"Wait. I've got a surprise for us," Gregory said. So off we went into the sewer. Once we arrived at our underground suite on Fourteenth Avenue, Gregory said "Okay Johnny, what's in the bag for today?" Johnny smiled triumphantly as he pulled a quart bottle of Ballantine beer out of his bag of tricks. That kid never ceased to amaze me.

"Wow, where'd you get it?" I exclaimed.

"It's my dad's. Swiped it from the fridge when my mom was watching *As the World Turns*." Johnny unscrewed the cap, took a swig and passed it to me. I took in a mouthful and immediately spat it out. This stuff tasted awful. How could my dad even drink a glass, let alone the two quarts a day which was rapidly becoming his custom?

"Come on, don't be a girl. Take a swig." So I tried again. This time I took a smaller mouthful and swallowed quickly before the bitter taste could linger. Whew! I couldn't see the attraction of this stuff, but I drank when it was my turn. Soon my head started to feel like it wasn't attached to my neck, and my stomach was burning. What was happening to me? Maybe this stuff was radioactive and I was going to turn green. We were living in the age of nuclear bomb shelters. The Cuban missile crisis was months away, but we knew there existed the threat of an invasion by something called "the Russians." I imagined Russians to be gigantic furry creatures with long snouts like elephant trunks, huge teeth like a snaggletoothed tiger and ugly claws. Maybe this beer stuff was turning me into one! I asked Gregory if I looked any different and he said no, I didn't, then asked me why. "Cause I feel funny, that's all," I replied. Maybe if I stood up I'd feel better.

I pushed myself off the rock with my hands and fell into the water. I couldn't stand up. I tried again and slipped again. Johnny and Gregory were laughing at me.

"You're just drunk, that's all," giggled Gregory.

What's drunk mean? My father drank this stuff all the time and he could stand up perfectly fine. Sometimes he talked really loud, but most of the time he just fell asleep in the living room chair.

"Here, eat some of my sandwich," Johnny handed me half of a bologna and mustard sandwich. Having the food in my stomach made me feel somewhat better. That Johnny sure was something, packing a sandwich to go with the beer. I ate the rest of the sandwich and tried standing up again. I was still a little shaky, but I could stand.

"Okay, let's get out of here and go to the creek," said Gregory.

I managed to stumble along the sides of the sewer, splashing into the water every now and then. I was wet anyway, so there was no point trying to stay dry. We walked through the open field to the creek and I tumbled in. The water was a little muddy colored—it had rained yesterday. I didn't care. I immersed myself, splashing the brown water on my face. The three of us were making quite a ruckus in the creek. We climbed out and took our wet clothes off, laying them over a rock to dry, and we lay on the grass baking in the sun. Johnny was jabbering about the Phillies. I didn't care about the Phillies. The National League was a foreign entity. Give me the American League and the Washington Senators. But the Senators were having a bad year (they went on to lose 101 games in 1962), and I found I had more to root for by switching my allegiance to Brooks Robinson and the Baltimore Orioles.

"So what's the big surprise?" I asked Gregory.

Gregory grinned and said, "Watch me." He stood up, buck naked and walked toward the creek bank. He disappeared for a moment. I didn't hear anything and I wondered if maybe he was all right when all of a sudden a brown monster appeared over the bank.

Johnny and I screamed and started to run when Gregory's voice said, "Hey, it's me, guys."

We stopped and looked at the brown creature. Maybe

the thing had eaten Gregory. That had to be it. There was no explanation for why Gregory's voice came from this thing, which had twigs and grass growing out of it.

"Hey, you guys, it's me. This is mud."

Upon closer examination, we discovered that it really was Gregory and he was covered head to toe with mud from the creek, with the twigs and grass thrown in for effect.

"Do I look scary?" he said, knowing that he had scared the bejesus out of us. Johnny and I nodded our heads, and then we made a beeline for the creek to apply some of that marvelous mud to ourselves.

After the three of us were encased in mud, Gregory said, "Let's sneak up on the girls around the block and make 'em scream." What a tremendous idea. Gregory really was the idea man in this outfit. He'd definitely have to get a job in the movies or in advertising when he grew up.

So off we went, three human mudpies stalking through the tall grass. When the mud began to dry, it took on a grayish tone, which made us look like zombies. Gregory was strutting along with his chest puffed out, admiring his handiwork. Just as we reached the end of the park, I realized that we had left our clothes drying on the rock. "Hey, we have to go back and get our clothes," I said. I couldn't go home naked without some sort of swift and terrible retribution awaiting me. We had these big old forsythia bushes in the back yard. The flowers were pretty yellow things, but we didn't have them for the flowers. Mom liked the branches, or "switches" as she called them. She'd take a couple of branches and let them cure on top of the icebox for a while. (While most of my backwoods Virginia-isms have long vanished, I still cannot call a refrigerator a fridge. It will always be an icebox to me.) When they had finished curing, they were ready to be used as instruments of torture. Thwack! across the back of the legs, amid cries of "please don't kill me," and "I'll be good from now on."

"We'll get 'em later. Come on, we're almost around the block," said Gregory. As usual, I capitulated to Gregory, which almost always got me in trouble. We stood behind Mrs. Bowden's house, which was on the corner of Fifteenth and Carlisle. Susie Crowe and Jane Tinsley were sitting on Jane's front step with their backs turned. A girl who lived three streets up, over on Twelfth Avenue, was there too. Her name was Joyce Irving. They had dolls strewn across the step. Susie and Jane were my age. Joyce was older, about eight I think. I didn't know what puberty was at the time, but I could see that Joyce's body was a little different from the rest of the girls. Her chest wasn't flat, which I found intriguing. I wondered what her chest looked like.

"Okay, let's sneak up on 'em," said Gregory. "I'll count to three. On three, let's run at 'em. And Johnny, yell as loud as you can. Like the monsters." Johnny had a voice like a bullhorn. Later he would grow up to make a living as a singer in a lounge band in Atlantic City. He definitely had a set of pipes.

"One, two...THREE!" We ran out from the bushes, yelling as loud as we could. Johnny was in great voice—his yell was as bloodcurdling as any monster I'd seen on our little black & white Philco. Jane, Susie, and Joyce screamed bloody murder, throwing their dolls up in the air as they started to run. We ran after them. Johnny was ad-libbing like a true master.

"I'm gonna eat you for dinner, I love to eat little girls," he yelled in that monster-loud voice. It had the desired effect because they were really screaming now and looking back over their shoulders in fright at the three mud monsters chasing them. It was a delicious moment. We were in our glory.

We chased them all the way up to Thirteenth Avenue. As we turned the corner of Thirteenth, we were met by a woman who I would find out later was Joyce's mom. This was not in the plan. She had an apron on and her arms were covered with flour and she held a rolling pin aloft like a hammer. I stopped and screamed. Johnny and Gregory kept running past her and they escaped. I was frozen in my tracks. "You'd better leave the girls alone," the Rolling Pin Woman said. I turned and started to run away, but I tripped on a crack in the sidewalk and fell to the concrete, scraping both knees and my elbow. As I lay there crying, the Rolling Pin Woman came over and said, "Are you okay, boy?" She knelt down and turned me over and said, "Why, you're a little girl!" I wondered how she knew this, and then she said, "Where are your clothes? Did those boys take them?" All of a sudden I remembered that I had nothing on except mud and twigs. I decided that it might be easier for me if I just played along with her, so I nodded my head and started crying again. She put her arms around me and helped me up and said, "You come back to our house and we'll fix you up." I liked the way she smelled, like warm bread. It felt good having her arms around me. I kept up the crying so she'd keep holding me. Maybe this was one of the benefits of being a girl.

She led me into the house through the back door. "Come on upstairs, honey, and let me wash those cuts," she said. I followed her through the downstairs. I was amazed at their house. My house was exactly like Johnny's and Gregory's houses—they were all pretty much the same on our block. This house was bigger. And they had a fireplace in their living room. As we went to the stairs, I saw Joyce peering out from the sun porch. She was making faces at me. I stuck out my tongue at her as I followed Rolling Pin Woman up the stairs.

She led me into the bathroom. "Joyce, come up here and help me," Rolling Pin Woman said. I heard footsteps on the hardwood stairs and Joyce's face appeared around the doorway. "Run a bath for our little friend here while I get her a towel and wash cloth." I sat on the toilet watching Joyce prepare a bath. "Okay, honey, why don't you get in the tub and I'll wash those cuts for you." I gingerly placed a toe in the water—ouch, it was hot! Joyce was getting even with me. I eventually made my way into the tub and sat down, feeling the clean hot water surround me. Mrs. Rolling Pin took a washcloth and started to rinse me off, then a loud buzzer rang. "Oh, it's my meat loaf. I've got to go turn it off. Joyce, would you finish washing her up for me while I finish making dinner? Your father will be home soon."

I shuddered thinking about how Joyce might further exact her revenge. She sat down on the edge of the tub and, to my surprise, she gently began to wash me. I winced when she got to my scraped knees, but she was very gentle. Until this point I had not uttered a word, but then she said to me, "Why do you hang out with those boys? They're bad and you're gonna turn out just like them." I informed her that I was really almost a boy, that I was just missing a piece and that I belonged with them, and she said, "Where are you from? You sure talk funny."

She was giggling. I thought she was laughing at me and I said, "I'm from Virginia and it's y'all who talk funny, not me. Whyn't you just leave me alone? I can wash myself." But she didn't leave. She stood up and started taking off her dress. "I'm coming in with you. Then you can wash me."

I sat in the lukewarm water staring at her as she removed her dress, then her undershirt. This was going to be an amazing experience, and one I was not sure I was prepared for. I couldn't take my eyes off her chest. She had tits! True, they were not anything like the ones I saw in Playboy, but it was a good start. My stomach started feeling funny again, like when I had drank the beer, only it was a different kind of funny feeling. This one was more enjoyable. She sat down opposite me in the tub and handed me the washcloth. I started to wash her. My stomach was getting worse. I wondered what was happening to me. Then Joyce said, "Do you like to play house?" I told her I did and that I always played the daddy. I wondered if she was going to ask me to play house. Then she said, "Pretend I'm the mommy and kiss me." I leaned over, stopped washing her and kissed her, a quick smack on the cheek. "On the lips," she said. As my lips met hers, my stomach did a flip-flop and my head started coming unglued from my neck. It felt like it anyway. Maybe now I was turning into a Russian. I didn't care. I liked the direction things were moving in.

I kept kissing her and then I made the mistake of placing my hand on her chest. Oh wow. My head must have fallen off. No, it was me losing my balance and falling into her. My head landed right on top of her breasts. I didn't know they were called breasts at the time, but I had one right on the tip of my tongue. My mouth was open and I didn't know what to do so I kissed it. Later on in life, it was revealed to me that I had been bottle fed, as lots of 50s children were, so I had never had the opportunity to develop a breast fixation as a child. I had a lot of catching up to do and I was making a herculean effort here in Joyce Irving's bathtub. And she seemed to like what I was doing so I kept it up.

All of a sudden, I heard a door slam shut and a

distinctly male voice boomed: "Honey, I'm home." We both sat up, startled into reality. She smiled at me and said, "We'd better get out of here." Both of us dried off quickly and then horror struck—I had no clothes! Joyce wrapped a towel around me and we went into her room where she pulled a dress out of her closet and said, "Put this on."

I recoiled as though I had just seen a werewolf and said, "I'd die before I put a dress on. Don't you have any jeans?"

"No, but my brother does." She went into his room and came back with an outfit I found much more acceptable. Except that her brother was ten, and his clothes hung on me like a sack. Still, it was better than a dress.

I stayed for dinner, at Joyce's mom's insistence. Joyce and I never spent another moment alone again, though I wanted desperately to. And I think she did too, but her dad got transferred shortly thereafter and they moved to someplace called Michigan. It may as well have been Russia as far as I was concerned. I moped around the house for weeks. My mother didn't quite know what to do to ease my misery, so she sent me off to Virginia to stay with my grandmother. Once there, I became even more morose as I realized how much I missed Pennsylvania. I couldn't lighten up enough to even play canasta with Grandma.

Then one day Grandma said to me, "Let's go downtown. There's a friend I want you to meet." Grandma was from England (she talked funny too) and she had had a lot of different jobs since coming to the United States. And she knew a lot of different people, so I went with her because I always liked the people she knew. They were strange but interesting.

We went up to this house and Grandma rang the doorbell. A tall, dark-haired man answered. He was a funny looking man because he had long hair like a woman. Grandma introduced me and said, "This is your Aunt Dallas." Aunt? I didn't know any Aunt Dallas. She did kind of look a little like my mom though. But Mom never mentioned Aunt Dallas. I wondered if Grandma was pulling my leg. Aunt Dallas was about six feet tall and built like, well, like a man. She didn't use nail polish and she smoked cigars. Grandma left me off and said she'd be back for me in a couple of hours. What in the world was Grandma doing, leaving me with this complete stranger?

Dallas took me into the living room where she had a card table set up. "Grandma tells me you like to play cards."

"That's right," I replied. "Canasta. Can you play?"

"Sure," said Dallas. She eased her long frame into a chair and motioned for me to do the same. "How 'bout a game?" she drawled. I nodded okay and she dealt.

We played cards for a while. She cleaned me out. Then she said, "Would you like a Coke?" I said yes and she said, "I'll be right back." She returned with two cokes and a photo album. I asked her what the pictures were of and she said, "You'll see." Now my curiosity was piqued. She spread the album out on the card table and we looked at the pictures. I recognized my mom in some and I pointed this out to Dallas. There were a couple of pictures of Dallas and Mom, and there were some other pictures of Dallas and some woman I didn't recognize. Since the woman kept appearing in a lot of pictures, I assumed it was a friend of the family.

Then Dallas said to me, "So tell me, do you have a boyfriend yet?" No one had ever asked me that. I was only accustomed to dealing with Gregory and Johnny and I didn't know how to respond to her. She put her hand on mine and said, "You can tell me." Well, there was something about the combination of her voice and her hand that made me feel okay. Like Mrs. Rolling Pin holding me. So I told her all about Joyce, and all about feeling different and feeling lousy that Joyce wasn't around. I even told her about the bathtub, though I left out the part about me kissing Joyce's boobs. I figured I was in enough trouble.

Dallas leaned back in her chair and put a cigar in her mouth. She lit the cigar. God, what a stink. To this day, I cannot tolerate cigar smoke. Then she blew a few smoke rings, which I found fascinating, and she said, "Don't ever feel bad about Joyce. And don't ever let anyone tell you you're different. You're no different than anyone else in the world. You don't have to be like anyone else. Remember that."

Then Grandma came and we left Aunt Dallas. Her

words played back and forth in my head like a broken record. And even though she told me I was no different than anyone else, in that summer of 1962 I realized that I was, because I liked girls and because I was one. In that summer, my questions about who I was were answered. I knew I wasn't a boy and that I never would be one. Because I liked being female. But what I liked even better were other females. And I had a whole lifetime to experiment.

Chocolate Cake

I love chocolate. Anything chocolate—M&Ms (my favorite candy), chocolate covered cherry cordials (I like the milk, but the dark's my fave), chocolate mousse, chocolate fudge ice cream…well, you get it now. Especially chocolate cake. The more chocolate, the more dark, the better!

So where was I? Oh yes, I love chocolate. Now what does this have to do with anything, you're asking? Well, there's always a story….

I recently had the occasion to take myself out to dinner. Not so special, really, but when you're used to eating with your lover every night and all of a sudden you're eating by yourself, well it's a bit of a shock to the system. She had to go out—without me!—for a business dinner meeting, and...well I was left to my own devices. I was given some money and told, "Now make sure you eat something, even if it's Burger King."

Well, I'm proud to say I did better than some fast-food grease pit. I decided to go into Philadelphia to a restaurant I'd heard a lot about in a very glitzy hotel and have myself a real honest-to-goodness gourmet dinner. Soup to nuts. And I don't eat much as it is, but I was a real gastro-glutton this night. I had Caesar salad for one, bread and butter, shrimp scampi on rice with garlic wine sauce. I was in the middle of sucking on a shrimp when I happened to glance up from my gluttony and notice this woman sitting two tables in front of me. She was staring right at me. At first I thought she was staring at me, that is, but then I realized that she was staring at my food.

She got up and walked towards me. She was taller than I, which isn't saying much (I'm 5'2"), but she had to be at least 5'8". And when you're my height, everyone looks six feet tall. What a gorgeous woman! Dark brown shoulder length hair that looked like, well, a river of chocolate. And what a bod... Anyway, she came toward me, pulled out the empty chair at my table, sat down, and in this unearthly, gorgeously Lauren Bacall-ish husky tone said, "I'm dying to know—what is that you're eating? It looks like shrimp scampi, but I couldn't tell from my table." What an introduction. I politely dabbed at my mouth with my napkin. How I managed to remember manners I will never know. And I replied, "It is scampi. You're very perceptive. Would you like a taste?"

Well, of course she did want some. Isn't that how all fantasies go? So I scooped up a nice fat forkful of shrimp and gathered up a heaping gob of rice with my spoon. I was going to put the contents on her plate and, I hoped, just sit back and watch her eat. She was gorgeous. I could pretend I was one of the shrimp. I began maneuvering both fork and spoon towards her plate. I am not very big and consequently am cursed with short arms, and so I could not reach her plate without standing up and leaning across the table. When I leaned over, my concentration was broken by the view I had of her breasts. A partial view, true, but it was enough. I could see the roundness, the beginning of nipple. But I needed a better vantage point. Maybe if I moved in closer. So I tried to stretch myself across the table even more. Being the extreme klutz I am, what else would have happened but that my fork full of shrimp fell out of my hand, clattering to the floor. I heard someone from the next table over remark, "How disgusting." Well yeah, honey, I hadn't planned on spilling it either. "Oh my God, I am sorry. What a klutz," I heard myself say. It was the end of my scampi. There was no more to give her, only my wimpy, wilted steamed broccoli. Yukkk. Well I could place another order for scampi. Hold on! It's $15.95 and I only had $30.00 to begin with. I hadn't even had dessert yet, which I cannot do without. Ahh, dessert. Salvation, maybe?

She must have been reading my mind, because she said, "It's okay. It's time for dessert and coffee. What do you think we should have for dessert? You choose."

So, what do I do? I'm here, alone in this great restaurant with this wonderful woman who wants me to order dessert and coffee for her. I hoped she liked chocolate. She had to. Chocolate…it has this rich sensuality, this allure to it. Most people that I know avoid it, because of diets, or the caffeine, or whatever. It's the ultimate, the forbidden, the one thing everyone dreams about when thinking of eating dessert. How many times have we all been at the office, listening to the late 40-ish, almost-menopause age, very much overweight women complain, "Oh, I'm on a diet, I couldn't possibly eat any of that," and then they take a piece, saying, "Well, just a small piece. I am on a diet, after all."

I can eat as much as I want of it because I never seem to gain weight. Working out like an Olympic hopeful five days a week helps. But it pays off because I get to have my chocolate. Well, back to the story. I regained my senses and looked back at this gorgeous thing at my table and said, "I'm going to have a look at the dessert tray, and then I can make up my mind about what to have. Would you also like some cappuccino?"

"Absolutely."

So I called the waiter over and asked to see the dessert tray. He brought it over immediately, it seemed, and I had the feast of the world before my eyes. German Chocolate (hmm), Black Forest (oohh), Chocolate

Cheesecake (yukk), Chocolate Mousse Pie (possibility), and then there was Chocolate Chip Supreme—it had a dark devil food cake with almost black chocolate icing inside and outside and semi-sweet dark chocolate chips imbedded within. A winner. I told the waiter we'd have two servings, but my new friend at my table said, "Just one serving. We'll share."

Our order was served. I got the cake and she got an empty plate. I said to her, "Mind if I try it first?" She shook her head of marvelous hair which I took as a yes and I dug in. It was absolutely delicious, the chocolate, and I could feel the instantaneous rush through my body, I suppose like a vampire feels the rush of the blood from his victim. It was exhilarating, addicting. No wonder people felt so strongly about chocolate. I sat back in my chair and sighed. Ahh, it was sinful. I closed my eyes for a moment and began imagining all kinds of things. But I had to share. I dug my fork in and carved out a nice big chunk of cake. I again tried to lean across the table, mindful this time of my previous unsuccessful effort, and I held the fork out and said something stupid. "Open wide, here comes your ecstasy." Ooooh. I have got to get better lines.

She opened her mouth, so wide that I could see she didn't have much dental work. But she was so beautiful I couldn't focus on her teeth. Again, I had the pleasure of viewing her cleavage, but from a much better position. But my innate clumsiness failed me again. I was so close to her, I looked down again and saw her nipples,

soft and brown, and I saw her entire breasts, the roundness and shadows descending below. As I strained
forward to see better, it happened again. I lost my
balance! I could feel myself falling, and I tried not to fall
onto the table. I succeeded and managed to fall onto the
floor next to the table where I had previously heard,
"How disgusting." This wasn't pretty. I was sprawled on
my back on the floor with my forkful of cake in one
hand and the other clutching the chair I had managed to
drag with me. I was so embarrassed. I wasn't hurt—just
the pride that made me do this stupid thing. I thought
about just turning over and crawling away on my hands
and knees when all of a sudden she was there, leaning
over me and offering me her hand, saying, "Are you all
right? Let me help you up." I accepted her hand, and
she said, "Let's get the dessert wrapped and go." So I
paid the check, got my cake in the customary Styrofoam
box and started for the door. I didn't even get to drink
my cappuccino. And I had paid $3.75 for it, plus $4.75
for the cake, tax and tip. I didn't have much left.

I was positive she wasn't coming. I knew a little
coffee shop where I could get my cappuccino cheap, so I
started out towards the lobby with my little Styrofoam
prize tucked under my arm. I heard the sound of heels
clicking against the marble of the lobby floor and I
heard her calling, "Wait! Don't go!" I kept going, trying
to lose her voice and knowing that if I heard her once
again I would stop and there was no telling what would
happen next. After all, I had a lover. I was committed,

though not trying very hard to continue to be so. Selfishly, I decided that I wanted my cake and to eat it by myself. So I marched on, my cake securely tucked in between my hand and my hip.

What happened next was totally unexpected. She ran up, planted herself in front of me and said, "I have a room. Let's go upstairs and have the cake and I'll order some cappuccino from room service." I tried to walk around her, but she placed a hand on my shoulder and said, "Let's go. Now." She was definitely the dominatrix type. I was playing the victim well, I suppose. I guess I could just go up, let her eat some cake and then go. Let them eat cake. It worked for Marie. Maybe it would work for me. It was good cake.

We stepped into the elevator and we rode up to the 35th floor. We'd have a very nice view of the city. Walking down the hall to her room, I again felt that twinge of guilt. What was I doing here? My lover was out having dinner with a bunch of stuffy old business people and here I was contemplating adultery with a stunning accomplice. It wasn't fair. We continued down the hall and she slid the keycard into the door, opened and beckoned, "Come in."

I followed her inside and my eyes feasted on the lavish surroundings: mirrored walls, plush carpeting. I peeked around and noticed the bath had a Jacuzzi. I vaguely heard her talking on the phone. She had a very nice situation for me to fall into. I walked over to the couch, sat down, and she slid beside me. "Well, let's have that cake. I've ordered cappuccino and ice cream from room service."

I fumbled with the lid and managed to retrieve the cake from the container. She took the cake from my hands, broke off a chunk and brought it to my lips. I devoured the cake and sucked on her fingers, licking every last drop of chocolate. There was a knock on the door. She got up and I heard her thanking the bellboy, and the door closed. "It's the ice cream and cappuccino," she said, and she reappeared with a container of Chocolate Cherry Cordial, a tray with two cups of cappuccino, whipped cream, a bowl of chocolate shavings and a very large spoon. She set the tray on top of the small dining table. "Let's eat."

She sat down on the couch next to me and proceeded to unbutton her shirt (no bra!). She removed her shirt and began to coat her torso with ice cream and cake. I was mesmerized by this sensual attempt at fresco (Michelangelo never had it so good), and I was so moved I buried my face in her breasts, in her chocolate covered breasts, and began to lick, to eat, until the chocolate was gone and there was only nipple. The nipple had some chocolate left so I sucked on the nipple until the chocolate was gone, while she moaned and writhed. Then she stood up and reached for the silver tray. "We need the cappuccino."

After she sat back down, she took off her remaining clothes. She sat down next to me, naked, and she took my hand in hers and said, "Make me cappuccino." I started to pick up the coffee cup, and her hand grabbed mine and she said more forcefully, "Make me feel cappuccino." Her hand gripping mine moved down between her legs. I felt the softness of her hair, her wetness. "Make me cappuccino—with whipped cream and chocolate," she said. I leaned down toward her legs when all of a sudden she jerked my head up, pulling my hair, which hurt tremendously. "No! Make me cappuccino, but tell me about it. Describe it. I want to imagine it."

I removed my hand from between her legs, and I took a spoon from the coffee tray and began to spoon whipped cream into my cup. "As I take this cream, I'm taking you. I move my lips against yours, I move my lips down your face, I feel your neck. I kiss your neck, your shoulders, and then I move toward your breasts." As I said these words, she sighed and moved toward me. "And now I'm at your breasts." I took a deep sip of the cappuccino. "I'm licking your breasts, pulling on your nipples with my teeth, biting you just a little, not enough to hurt but enough to make the liquid flow between your legs."

She moves on the couch, arching her back so that her breasts stand up firmly. I am ready now. I move in toward her and her hand stops me. "No. Tell me." I stop, dumbfounded. What else can I tell her? Just tell her as if it's happening. So I do.

"I suck on your nipples, I take my hand and put it between your legs and feel the softness, the wetness. You open your legs and I can see your cunt. Waiting for me."

"Take the cream," she says. "Spread it on me."

I take the cream, spreading it between her legs, on top of her rich mound of hair. I sprinkle the chocolate shavings on top of the cream, and I bend down to eat. Licking the cream, then I taste the chocolate, and finally I begin to taste her. "Now pour the coffee on top of my cunt," she says. Pour the coffee? But won't it burn? "Do as I say." So I reach up and grab the silver container, twisting the lid, and then I gingerly pour a small stream onto her. She winces a bit, and she grabs my hair, hurting me a bit, and says, "Here's your cappuccino." I dive in, licking the coffee mixed with cream mixed with chocolate mixed with her come (and she is coming in a big way), and I can't get enough. I pour more hot coffee, she screams a bit, and I spoon more whipped cream and chocolate and I keep licking. And licking and licking, and I can feel her move into me, her cunt in my face, and I cannot stop myself, I grab her legs and hold her to myself, bringing her cunt into my face and I go completely crazy on her, licking and sucking. She is dripping wet, coming all over my face, liquid running down my chin, and I sit up, exclaiming, "Something's missing!"

I lean over her naked and beautiful body, reaching for the remnants of the ice cream (now sadly melted) and the leftover cake. I sit down and smear the cake and a handful of ice cream on her cunt and dive in.

Never had I tasted anything so good. Chocolate come.

How divine. I kept going, going until all of her limbs spasmed, and she shook as though having a fit and said no more and I knew it was no more. She was spent, completely exhausted. I had never made anyone come like that. She sat up, looked at her watch. It was the only thing she had on. Then she said, "It's time for you to go."

Time? Who had a thought about time? I started to protest, as I was incredibly turned on and was hoping she'd reciprocate the cappuccino making (we could have more cake and leave out the coffee—I have a low pain threshold), but she gently pushed me away and said, "You have to go. I'm expecting my husband at any moment."

"Will I see you again?"

"You'll know where to find me—I love chocolate cake and cappuccino."

So I left, bewildered, bewitched, bedazzled and a little bit sad. After all, this had been a most incredible experience. I started thinking about how I would explain this to my lover—I hadn't washed up and I probably had chocolate stains on my shirt, for godsakes! What had been an evening of astounding highs was quickly becoming one major depression for me.

I entered the cab, gave the driver my address and we were off. It seemed like we flew to my little row house and still I had not thought of a plausible lie to tell my lover. I paid the cabbie with my last $2 including tip and I put my key in the deadbolt. As I opened the door, my lover walked into the dining room from the kitchen. She was putting wine glasses back into the china cupboard and though she knew I was there she wasn't looking at me.

"How was dinner? Where did you go?"

"I went to the Bellevue."

"The Bellevue! Well, I'm proud of you. What did you have for dinner?"

"Shrimp scampi."

"And for dessert?"

"Chocolate Chip Supreme."

"I might have known." As she walked into the living room to embrace me, she stopped dead, looked at me and said, "What the hell happened to you?" Looking down at myself, my worst fears were realized. I had chocolate on my shirt, chocolate on my hands. I raised my hands and ran my fingers around my mouth and discovered sticky chocolate smears all around my lips. Plus I probably smelled like cunt to boot. I thought I'd have a heart attack. Well, better to tell the truth since I couldn't think of a believable enough lie. "Well, there was this woman and she made me go back to her room and eat chocolate cake with her and she took off all her clothes and spread the cake all over her and I ate it off her and made her come."

She put her hands on her hips, tilted her head in that funny way that I love so much and started to laugh. "That's the best one yet. I swear you come up with the best stories. I know you too well, my little klutz. You're just too embarrassed to tell me you tripped and fell into the dessert table." I laughed, probably a little too much, and I shifted my feet. "You'd better go upstairs and get those clothes into some cold water in the sink. And wash up. I'm not going near you until you do."

After I regained my sense of feeling in my legs, I started for the stairs and said, "You know me too well."

She smiled and said, "I just made some coffee. Want some?"

Fire Escape

It was just another Friday night in another smoky bar in some stupid little town where the locals get to go out twice a week. My bandmates and I had arrived at 7:30 to set up all our equipment. Unfortunately, the bar scene doesn't really pay like it used to, and we could not afford roadies, so we did all the moving ourselves. And what a bitch it was, up two flights of a fire escape! (The owner did not want the dinner crowd disturbed so we had to use it). Of course all our equipment is antiquated, meaning large and heavy, so it's always a workout just setting up. Fridays are the tough days, since we all leave work and come straight to the bar and we're always beat from working nine to five. Not that I'm complaining...but we're not getting any younger.

We're a five piece band, and I'm the bass player. Years ago, when I started playing, it was always unusual to see female musicians. I used to hear all the classic lines: "You're pretty good for a girl," and "Who taught you to play bass—your boyfriend?" and so on. Now it's different, what with the emergence of players like Melissa Etheridge, Lita Ford, Vixen. Now there's a band that can play. And Joan Jett. So people don't gawk at me so much now, which is fine with me.

We were all set up and sound checked when I decided it was time to change into my "stage" clothes— really nothing more than an old faded pair of jeans with gaping holes in the knees, a tank top and a paisley vest. But I was dripping with sweat from the set-up and smelled like the Dumpster out back. At least I would smell better when I washed up, dumped some powder on and put the clean clothes on. I walked into the ladies room with my gym bag and my hanging clothes. Not being the exhibitionist, I always use a stall to at least change my underwear and shirt, then I can move out into the main area to do the rest. The stalls are very cramped. I stood at the sink and washed up with the standard dispenser liquid soap which always makes you smell like a cheap whore, and I was reaching for my clothes so I could enter a stall when the main door banged open and a tall woman pushed past me into the stall I was going to use! I immediately looked under the door of the other stall and saw a pair of Doc Martens. Rats! I was left to change completely in the main area. Oh well. Not much time. I would have to hurry.

I stripped my shirt off, sprinkling baby powder all over my chest and stomach, then put on my tank top. I removed my sneakers and sweat pants, taking off my panties and sprinkled some powder down there, and stepped into a pair of fresh underwear. As I was pulling them up, the door of the other stall opened and the Doc Martens stepped out. I froze, with my underwear at my ankles. As I looked up from the Doc Martens, I saw baggy pants, suspenders, a white tux shirt opened to the cleavage, long dirty blonde hair and an intelligent, gorgeous, sensuous face with high cheekbones, slightly parted wet lips and eyes as wide as mine.

"Oops, I'm sorry. I didn't know you were changing," the sensuous lips said.

"It's okay," I mumbled. "I'm in the band and I have to get ready."

"Great. I'm here with some friends. I'll see you out there." She gave me a long glance up and down my body and left, and I let out a huge breath and quickly pulled the underwear up, put the jeans on, and the vest, smeared some basic makeup on and got the hell out of Dodge before someone else came in. I tell you, it's rough being a star....

Once the room lights go down and the stage lights go up, it's always hard to see the crowd. And Sandy, our light person, sometimes she blinds me with a spot when it's my turn to sing. Sometimes it's so blinding I can't see my fretboard and I wind up on the wrong string or wrong fret, making a stupid mistake and having to bear the piercing glare of everyone else in the band. And tonight was no exception. We do 75 percent original stuff and the rest covers. I do very little singing (even on my own tunes), with the exception of the Melissa Etheridge stuff we do. I have the voice for it—raspy, Rod Stewart-ish, and it suits me. We were into our first set (we only do three) and I had just finished, "Bring Me Some Water," and I was blinded by the lights as usual and made two mistakes—hitting the D string instead of the A string, which wasn't too bad, and hitting a C instead of a B which sounded absolutely awful. Whew! Glad that was over. One more tune and we're done for this set. I had been glancing around the room periodically to see if my bathroom friend was there, but I really couldn't tell, what with the lights and all. And the smoke—it was awful. A complete haze of fog. Some nights I would be gasping for air because of the thick cloud of smoke in the room. I was sure that after ten years in clubs I was going to die of lung cancer and no cigarette ever having touched my lips—just second hand smoke.

We finished the last song of the set and I took my bass off, wiping the strings down—the sweat from my hands was unbelievable that night. I felt all sticky, icky from having sweated so much, so I headed for the bathroom to wash off. The line for the bathroom was way too long, and I pushed open the back door to go up the fire escape to the employee bathroom—bathroom being a joke name for the room. There was a six foot hole in the floor where there once had been a tub—the electrical wiring was an omnipresent octopus as there was no wall material at all—just studs—and when you flushed the toilet, it flushed hot water! A true hot seat. Well at least the walk up the fire escape would cool me off.

As I walked out the door toward the fire escape, I heard a female voice: "Hey, bass player." I turned around and saw my friend from the bathroom, the one who eyed me up and down as I stood with my pants down. "Caught you with your pants down, didn't I?" she said with a smirk. I felt my face flush and I tried to fight off my increasing attraction by displaying a sudden rush of fake anger. "What's it to you?" I said. "You like what you saw. You like girls, maybe?" That'll either scare her away or make her come back with a zinger, I thought. I was expecting her to back off, but she threw me a screwball with: "Maybe I do." Strike two.

Wait a minute, she didn't really look like she'd go… Well, nobody looks like they're supposed to look anymore. And I was feeling very turned on. So I decided to encourage her. "Maybe you do, maybe you don't. You don't look like a girl who likes girls." Let's see what she's made of. "Try me," was the reply. Here we go, tit for tat.

"What makes you think I like girls," was my reply. All

right, I made it a full count. Let's see what she does with this one. She came back with a fastball: "You don't just like girls. You want pussy." Oooh, a heavy hitter. Here I am, standing out on the fire escape, haggling with a very attractive woman in baggy pants, suspenders, and Doc Martens, who is trying to convince me of my own sexual persuasion. I give up, she wins.

"Okay, you're right. So now that we've made this big discovery, what do we do about it?" I said, looking at my watch. We had wasted ten minutes verbally sparring and I had twenty to go. I still had to pee and wash up and try to get a Guiness Stout before the next set.

"Why don't I follow you upstairs and we can discuss it," she purred, sipping on her Coors Light. Ugggh, light beer. If I'm having a beer, it's gotta be a good one, like a Guiness. Well, we can overlook some things, can't we?

So I turned and started up the fire escape and I heard her clanking right behind me. We reached the top, I opened the door, and we went into the storage room where the "bathroom" was. Back with the shelves of maraschino cherries and green olives. What a great place to conduct an affair, or whatever it was we were about to have. I wasn't totally sure. I turned to face her and she came right up to me and said: "I couldn't help myself in the bathroom when you were changing. I was watching you from the crack in between the door, and when I came out I knew you wouldn't have your pants on." So she had spied on me! "Well, of all the noyve," I tried in my best fake New Yawk Jewish accent, and she laughed.

"It's just like a dyke wannabe to pull this shit, hiding in women's bathrooms, spying on dykes as they perform the most basic bodily functions, just to get a cheap look," I continued, and I had her rolling now. She was bent over, laughing, and I was laughing with her as I thought about the scene in the bathroom and how I must have looked with my pants around my ankles. I was still laughing when she stopped laughing, moved toward me and kissed me, full on the lips, right there in front of the maraschino cherries. I kissed her back, our tongues touched and I had this feeling, like maybe she was for real. I decided to find out. But I had to hurry—I only had fifteen minutes till the next set.

I pulled her back toward the end of the shelves, where they kept the top shelf liquor (this place never served top shelf, mind you—this place was cheap) and where it wasn't so light and wasn't so prone to employees poking around. They wouldn't be looking for top shelf, now would they? I gallantly threw my vest down and cleared a spot on the floor of dust (dirt I couldn't do anything about) and we lay down. She was kissing me, touching me all over, and I was feeling very hot and pressed for time. I told her: "I don't have much time." She said, "Okay. Let's go." And we did. She tore at my tank top, ripping it out of my jeans, pushing it over my head and diving right into my breasts. I threw aside her suspenders and fumbled with the buttons of her tux shirt until I got frustrated and tried to pull it over her head. She stopped and helped me, and soon we were both naked from the waist up. I sucked her nipples hard, and they grew taut and erect under my tongue. She had her hand in my jeans, feeling the moistness in my cunt and massaging me. I plunged my hand inside her pants, feeling the silkiness of her underwear. I pushed them aside and I found her cunt, soft, moist, ready. I withdrew my hand and with both hands I began unzipping her pants frantically. She helped me push the pants and her underwear down her legs, down to her ankles. I moved on top of her, my breasts touching hers, feeling the unique sensation of nipple on nipple. She was unzipping my jeans and her hand was moving into my cunt. I gently pushed her away and moved my head down between her legs, my tongue finding her wet and inviting. I licked her and sucked her clit, gently rubbing my tongue against it at first, then I went harder and faster, sucking and licking, every now and then biting just a little. She moaned and moved into me and I went into her more, immersing myself in her. She was wet and sticky and she flowed onto me, onto my face, all over me and then she went into a sort of rhythmic spasm with even more flowing out of her and all of a sudden it was over. She collapsed on the floor and I with her. I laid my arms across her and held her, kissing her face, her lips, and just wanting to stay with her all night when all of a sudden I heard a voice break the reverie saying, "Hey Kim! You up here? Time to go on!" I sat up, shaken by the intrusion. I looked at my companion on the floor and said, "I've got to go on for the next set."

She lay there, naked and lovely and swooning, and she said, "I'll wait for you. How long will you be?"

I said, "One hour set, thirty minute break. Put your shirt on, pull your pants up and come downstairs. I wouldn't want anyone else to find you. I'll get you something to drink so you don't have to pay." Normally, I would have been surprised at my philanthropy, but not after this experience.

I waited until she was dressed and then we left, my jeans dripping and my heart pounding, knowing that my fingers would fly through the next hour of boring songs mistake-free, uncomplaining until they could touch what awaited me at the top of the fire escape.

The Shiner

I was standing by the cigarette machine, minding my own business, feeling sorry for myself that no one was attempting to disturb me. I'd been to this bar a couple of times before, usually with a group of friends, but never on my own. I always had my gang to look after me—Hey, Kate needs a drink... Hey Kate, wanna dance? By now, you have surmised that I'm unattached and the fifth wheel most of the time. Tonight I was on my own and things weren't looking very good. For one, I was always in the background with Roxy, Mary Lou Who, Sharon EW (EW for Evil Wicked—more about that in another story) and Weezie around. They had the dominant personalities, they bellied up to the bar and ordered all the drinks, booked their dance partners. Hell, they even had creative nicknames. "Kate" kind of pales in comparison with "Weezie."

Well, the gang went to a Bette Midler concert, and since I can't stand her I resisted their pleading with me to go. Tonight I needed to find out if I could stand alone and not in their collective shadow. So off I went to the Den of Iniquity. Well, the score so far: Bette Midler 4, Kate 0. I was even having trouble getting the bartender's attention. Being short and all, I had to practically stand on the bar waving my $20 bill like a flag before I got served. And then she looked at me like, "Who the fuck are you?" Sigh. It can only get better, right? Wrong.

Some big bulldyke who wasn't watching where she was going ran smack into me, pushing me into the wall and knocking my nice, cold, Beck's Dark out of my hand and onto the floor where the beer foamed up nicely and the bottle shattered. Of course, she didn't even stop to apologize—must have been a hot one waiting. Probably didn't notice me. At first I just stood there morosely, watching the coat chick sweep up the glass shards into the dustpan. Then it hit me. She ran into me. I was there first.

A tiny little fuse went off in my head. I nervously walked over to her table where she was seated with some other smaller versions of herself and a couple of cute femmes and I tapped her on the shoulder and said,

"Excuse me, but you bumped into me back behind the bar and spilled my entire beer all over me and the floor." She turned around and stood up—boy, she was HUGE—and said: "Do I know you?" in a basso profundo voice that made my legs feel like jelly. "Well, I usually come here with Weezie, Mary Lou Who, Roxy and Sharon." She glared at me, then glanced at her compatriots and said, "Girlfriends, does this little asswipe look like someone that Weezie and Roxy would let hang out with them?" I watched them all shake their heads "No," each with a silly smirk on their faces. "So this is how it's gonna be," I thought. This bar wasn't going to be a place I could just hang out by myself. I need to find another place and make my own mark. Without the rest of the gang.

I was jolted out of my thought process by a large hand on my shoulder. I looked up. It was BigDyke and she was talking to me. "Did you hear me, you little cuntface? I said to go the hell home and leave us alone." The little fuse in my head began to burn brighter, and all of a sudden it blew up. Or rather I did. I grabbed at BigDyke's hand on my shoulder and said, "Take your goddamn hand off of me. And don't ever call me cuntface, you big fat elephant-swine gorilla-dyke. Hell yeah, I'm leaving. Who wants to be in a room with the likes of you?"

And as the last word escaped my lips, her fist caught my left cheekbone, right under my eye socket. I took off like a rocket and landed on the floor on my back and my head smacked the floor next to someone's shoe. Ohhhh, the pain—I was not only seeing stars, I was feeling them, their little points digging into each nerve in my face, into my eye. My eye! I could see at first, but then it seemed like my field of vision was getting smaller, like the lens of a camera closing. And now I couldn't see! What did she do, blind me? I reached my hand up to my cheek and felt a golf ball growing right under my eye. No, wait, it was becoming a baseball! My eye was swelling shut; that's why I couldn't see. I was gonna have a major shiner from this one, baby.

Someone helped me up—I don't know who and I was being escorted to the door. A slightly disembodied voice said, "I saw what happened when she ran into you, but you shouldn't mess with Big Jean, she has a bad temper." Yeah, I found that out. At least the doorwoman was nice enough to give me back my cover charge, seeing the misery I was in and I hadn't even been there fifteen minutes. Another kind soul placed a napkin with some ice cubes in my hand and said, "Keep this on your eye—try to keep the swelling down. She really caught you with a good one." Oh well. I guess I'll never have to worry about a career as a boxer—I wouldn't last thirty seconds in the ring.

God, I hurt. Everywhere. I think she broke every bone in my body. As I made my way down the stairs, holding onto the handrail with my right hand and the iced napkin clumped under my eye with my other hand, I stopped and fumbled in my pocket for my keys. My keys! They weren't in my coat! I tentatively walked back up the stairs and the doorwoman said, "You can't come back in—you're history." I said, "I'm really sorry but I think my car keys fell out of my coat when she hit me. Could I just go in and look for them?"

"No way, sweetheart. If I let you in and Big Jean sees you, your face will be hamburger in two seconds. Not that it looks real good right now. Why don't you go across the street to the Savoy and wait, say twenty minutes? Big Jean don't stay long on Saturday night—she likes to make a show at every joint in town on Saturday. When she leaves, I'll look for them. What kind of car key is it and what's the chain look like?" I described my key chain and keys and pleaded with her to find them, since my house keys were on the chain too. My life was on that key chain, and it was lying somewhere near Big Jean's feet. And now I hear that Big Jean goes to every joint in town. What kind of chance did I have now of making it on my own? I'd have to move out of town.

I went back down the stairs, my face throbbing and the ice melted in the napkin. Maybe I should go to the hospital. At least there I could get some kind of treatment and some sort of painkiller. But then I realized I didn't have my insurance card with me, only my money and driver's license. Guess the Savoy was the logical choice. Maybe if I sat in the back no one would notice that Cyclops was making a special appearance at the Savoy Coffee Shop—Tonight and only Tonight! Live and In Person—the one and only Lesbian Cyclops!

I slinked in the front door and hallelujah! there was a booth in the very back. I slid in with my back facing outward. My God, the planets must have realigned. My luck was changing. Someone had left a copy of today's newspaper on the seat! I would be able to hide my face in the paper. I quickly put the paper up and glanced over my shoulder to see who was in the room. There were a couple of old queens at the counter, some lipstick lesbos in one booth near the front, and a waitress who looked like Bea Arthur from *Golden Girls*, only a little younger. The waitress came over and said, "Can I getcha coffee?"

I didn't look up from my paper and mumbled, "Coffee is fine. And could I have a large glass of ice, please?"

"What's that, honey, I didn't hear ya?"

I peered up from the paper and said, "A large glass of ice."

She stared at my face and bellowed in a voice loud enough to drown out Ethel Merman, "Honey, what the hell happened to ya?" She turned and motioned towards the kitchen, "Hey Mary, bring me some ice in a towel. Hurry it up, will ya?"

I was embarrassed by the commotion because now the entire room was looking my way. I felt like crawling into a hole and never coming out. Just as I was mentally crawling into the hole, I heard Bea Arthur say, "Okay Mary, would you mind taking care of her? My number three's up." Bea Arthur left and when she moved I saw this dark-haired woman with big brown eyes, full ruby lips and a body like Venus de Milo (with arms and a lot less in the hips) standing there with a dirty towel full of ice. I couldn't believe my luck, or lack of it. Just when I was the second coming of Cyclops, the most gorgeous girl in the entire universe was waiting to give me ice. My life had to be cursed somehow.

The archangel Mary stood looking at me in disbelief, the water from the melting ice dripping from the towel down her arm. I tried to smile (it hurt!) and said to her, "I don't always look this good. You should see me on a bad day." She started laughing and said, "Forgive me. Here's some ice. Does it hurt very much?" Ahhh, her voice was melodic, enchanting. I was beginning to forget how much pain I was in. And so infatuated was I that I blurted out, "Doesn't hurt so much now that you're here." Ooooh. I'd like to take that line back, please. Too late. What if she wasn't even gay? Well, she had surely run into enough of my ilk in this part of town. As attractive as she was, she had to be used to dykes coming on to her. She was still smiling, though. It's possible that she was feeling sorry for the village idiot who got run over by Big Jean's fist.

"Can you drive? I mean, can you see enough to drive? Your eye is practically shut, you know."

"Well, now that you mention it, I can't see. And even if I could, my car keys are across the street upstairs somewhere on the dance floor. The doorwoman said she'd bring them over when Big Jean left."

"Big Jean? Is she the one who did this to you? You're not the first one I've seen get creamed by Jean." Ahhh, she was familiar with the work of Big Jean. Perhaps I was not the first person she had served ice to.

Mary stood there with her hands on her hips, frowning. "You've got to get home and keep ice on that eye. We've got to get your keys and get you home." Uh, what did she say? We? All of a sudden I was not in this alone. I had become a We. Things were beginning to look up. As if there had been any other way things could have gone. Certainly not any further down or I'd be looking for the nearest bridge. That is, if I could see the nearest bridge. "Wait, I'll be right back," my guardian angel said, and then she was gone, disappearing into the kitchen. Probably had another order to get out. Somebody would be very angry about their scrambled eggs being late.

Magically she reappeared within moments. "I took the rest of the night off. I'll make it up later in the week. Let's go find your keys." And off we went, the angel and Cyclops, stumbling across the street and up the stairs into the scene of my most recent nightmare. Wisely, I waited in the stairwell, lest the doorwoman or Big Jean catch sight of me. I decided to let Mary handle this one. My eye continued to throb and I became aware of a very bad pain in the back of my head right where I had hit the floor. Tomorrow would be a good day to just stay in bed. The thought of lying in my little bed sounded too good to be true right now. I wondered if I would even see my homely abode tonight. And then it hit me, the pain I was in, the emotional pain I felt. Not just from being hit. The pain of being alone, away from my friends. Especially the pain of always being the tag-along fifth wheel. "There must be a reason why I still don't have anybody" I thought, fighting a wave of self-pity. And there must be a reason why tonight's events happened. I am a believer in fate. If nothing else, I would learn something from this. "Yeah, I'll learn not to come in here without a bodyguard," I whispered out loud, and started laughing to myself.

"Found 'em!" shouted Mary as she bounded down the steps towards me, my keys dangling from her fingers as she held her hand high like a hunter displaying the spoils of the hunt. My spirits lifted as she drew next to me. She smelled like the kitchen at the Savoy, true—all bacon and eggs—but underneath the kitchen odor she smelled like perfume too. Something Estée—White Linen, White Satin—I never was good with perfume names.

"Where's your car?" Mary said as we walked out the door. I directed her to the parking lot around the corner. "And it's a red Nissan, right?"

Right again. "It's five speed. Can you drive stick?"

Mary stopped and looked at me. "No, I can't," she said. "I never learned how."

Well, this would be an interesting ride home….

We entered the car with me in the driver's seat. It was decided that I would shift gears and work the pedals and Mary would steer. I could see well enough with one eye to know when to put the brakes on, hopefully. Miraculously, we made it home without a hitch, save for a big pothole that Mary didn't steer clear of and I ran over at full speed. A front end alignment was definitely in the cards.

We pulled up outside of my house and I started to put the car in gear and apply the emergency brake. Uh oh—how was Mary going to get home? I posed the question to her and she said she didn't know, she'd have to take a cab. "But a cab is expensive. It'll cost you at least $20.00. Not at this time of night—I wouldn't feel right sending you home in a cab. You never know what kind of loonies there are out there. Why don't you stay over? I have a sofa-bed you can sleep on."

Mary agreed to accept my hospitality and together we walked up the front steps, up the stairs, finally to the third floor and through my front door, after some fiddling with the lock.

My apartment is not a castle. But it is located within a gorgeous old three story home on Spring Garden Street not too far from the Art Museum. There are five apartments in my building and all have magnificent twelve foot ceilings, large windows that paint the floor with sunshine, and nice old baths with little tiny white tiles and old pedestal sinks. Mary was having a field day oohing and ahhing at all my fine architectural details, but at this point all I was interested in was the ice tray in the refrigerator, the glasses in the top cabinet and the bottle of Chivas in the bottom cabinet.

I poured two glasses for us without even asking Mary

if she liked Scotch. If she didn't drink it I would, the pain was so bad. Mary handed me a Tylenol with codeine that I had left over from my last root canal. Then I lay down on the couch, chased my Tylenol with a very long swig and closed my eyes. Ahhh, the pain…was still there. Well, let's try another long swig. I was so focused on killing my pain that I didn't notice the hand on my leg. What hand? Must be Mary. What's Mary doing? I opened my eyes and saw her, my angel, sitting very close to me with her hand on my thigh. "Are you okay?" she whispered. Her hand moved from my leg to my face, caressing me softly, slowly. This was too good, had to be a dream, right?

I said, "Doctor Chivas is fixing me right up with some assistance from Nurse Tylenol." She looked so beautiful right now. Then I added, "And a major part was played by Chief Cook and Ice Maker Mary—I don't even know your last name." The Chivas was taking hold. I was very relaxed and the pain was getting further away.

Mary leaned over and kissed me lightly, right behind my ear. Then she whispered in my ear "Angelo." I repeated this and asked her what it was. She said, "It's my last name." Angelo. Angel.

"You really are an angel then," I said, my hands moving up to caress her face. She was very soft. And so beautiful. I had been going to bars for years and never had I seen a creature like this in a bar. Maybe I was learning something. To stay out of bars in the future perhaps. And to avoid the Big Jeans of the world.

Her lips were on mine, soft and sweet. I could not believe this was happening. After all those Saturday nights wasted with Weezie and the gang, never meeting anyone I could be semi-interested in, here she was, right in my house, on my couch. Kissing me. With my new Cyclops face. If she could love me looking like this... I was in my own private heaven right now. She wouldn't even have to make love to me. Just stay with me, holding me, letting me look at her. That's all I wanted.

And that's all I got. Mary stopped kissing me, and said to me, "It's not right for me to be doing this when you're not feeling well. But I want to stay with you. Maybe tomorrow you'll feel better."

She was right. I had downed her Scotch as well as my own, and coupled with the codeine-laced Tylenol, my vision in my one good eye was pretty fuzzy. She got me up off the couch, we walked slowly to the bedroom. She undressed me down to my undershorts and tank top, pulled the covers back and I slid into the cold sheets. I was half asleep when I felt the bed move slightly and I knew she had lain down next to me. Then her arms were around me, and we both fell fast asleep.

The next morning I woke with a hangover (I never was much of a Scotch drinker/codeine abuser) and my eye looked absolutely stunning. From a horror movie special effects-makeup standpoint, that is. But the pain had lessened somewhat. I took two regular Tylenol, and returned from the bathroom. Mary was still there, under the covers, sleeping. I hadn't dreamed it—she really had spent the night. I slid beneath the sheets, trying not to disturb her. I thought about what lay ahead of me. Should I call a cab for her, send her home? After seeing how horrible I looked, I had lost whatever confidence I had gained last night. Maybe I should just wait until my face was normal and then we could try and have a date or something. With my luck though, she would meet someone else while I was recovering. I started to move toward the next thought, the obvious end-of-this potential-love-connection. Then her hands were around my waist, moving beneath my underwear. I turned around and faced her. She was wide awake, looking just as gorgeous if not more gorgeous than last night as she kissed me. A long, lingering, tongue-in-search-of-another kiss. I could feel strange things happening to my body—pulse quickening, feeling very warm all of a sudden. Then I remembered and said, "Are you blind or are you just ignoring my face?"

She responded by moving her hand around down inside my underpants, making me crazy, and said, "I'm not thinking about your face. Your face will get better. And so will you. There are other body parts that interest me right now." She lifted my tank top with her other hand and her lips were on my breast, and suddenly I didn't care about my face either. My face? My face could wait. This, on the other hand, could not.

Tools of the Trade

I was late, as usual. Late with everything—late getting up in the morning, late getting to work, late going to a meeting, late coming back from the meeting. And because I was up against a major deadline, I would be late leaving the office tonight. Same old story—me, my slooow Mac IIci and my drafting table. Not my idea of a hot threesome. If this was going to be the extent of my life, I'd better start getting a new one, preferably with a warm body and not the tools of the trade.

After a few hours of electronically cutting, pasting, typesetting and scanning, I was tired and ready for a break. I still had at least another hour to go before these ads would be ready. It was 7:30 P.M. when I walked into the kitchen and smelled the coffee. It was burning. No, it was beyond burning. It had solidified. Disgusted, I turned the burner off, put the pot in the sink and filled it up with water. This would have to sit overnight before it could even be washed. Doesn't anybody ever keep an eye on this stuff? We could have had a fire in here.

I decided on a Pepsi and went back into my office. The building seems so strange at night—so quiet and empty, save for the familiar hum of the idle copier and the occasional ringing of the fax machine. Even now, at 7:30, the faxes were coming through. None for me, thank God. I was determined to get finished, go home and have a nice hot bath and some wine and then crash-hhh...and get up late tomorrow and start the whole draining cycle all over again.

My eyes were glued to the monitor, and I was so engrossed in thought that I didn't hear the footsteps until it was too late, and then I heard a voice ask me: "Are you using the copier?" Startled, I jumped literally out of my seat. Turning around, I saw the body attached to the voice. And what a body—slim hips, gently swelling breasts, and a face that would be very nice to come home to. Her face looked vaguely familiar. She must have noticed me staring, because she said, "Are you okay?" Instantly I snapped to attention and said, "I'm sorry. I was really concentrating and you startled me."

She said, "I don't think we've met. I'm Karen Myers. I work on the first floor for James Engineering."

Ah, I knew I had seen her in the building before. It's a big building and one runs into a lot of faces. A lot of faces easily forgettable. But not this face. I introduced myself and said, "Now, what did you ask me?"

She said, "I wanted to know if you were going to use the copier because I have a big job to run off and I didn't want to tie it up if you needed it. Normally when I have a run this large, I stay late and do it since no one's usually here at this hour. What are you doing here this late?"

I told her about my horrible day and the deadlines I had to meet and how I wasn't quite finished. This advertising business, somedays it's a killer. I then told her I wasn't using the Xerox machine and she could duplicate, collate, staple—whatever—to her heart's content. She thanked me and left. Shortly thereafter, I heard the familiar grinding of the machine as it cranked out the big copy job. Someday we'll have to get a new machine. This one's only three years old and it breaks down every month because it gets so much abuse. But, hey, it's not my company....

I put my nose to my desktop grindstone and soon I could see the finish line ahead. I popped a couple of photos in the scanner, cleaned them up a bit with my image editing software, and pasted them into the next ad in my Pagemaker. I was on my last ad! Hallelujah! I laid out my page, loaded some images from my CD

ROM drive, and was just starting to set the type when she appeared in my office again.

"Something's wrong with the Xerox—it keeps jamming. Do you know anything about it?"

I'm somewhat the "machine geek" around these parts—whatever breaks, I get the call to fix it. Sighing internally at having to delay finishing my ad, I said, "Sure, I'll look at it," and got up and followed her down the hall. Watching her from behind, I was able to further appreciate her physical assets. And she did have some ass...ets. I was beginning to enjoy the delay she was causing.

I opened both doors—what a mess. Paper jammed in every part. I opened a few of the problem areas and was able to get some of the jammed papers out. But the rest were just too crumpled up and they were lodged so tightly in the parts. I tried to get to them but—ouch! The metal blazing hot from all that copying. There was no way I could do anything, especially with the machine that hot, and I explained this to Karen. She stood there with a frown and said, "Well, so much for staying late to get this done. I guess this will have to wait until tomorrow."

I told her that even after the machine had overnight to cool off that it still might need to be serviced by a repairman, which might mean a further setback. "You might want to check out Kinko's—they're open twenty-four hours. That is, if your boss will spring for it."

She looked at me and said, "What choice does he

have? You're a genius!" She gave me a little hug which I found surprising and a bit exciting, and then she said, "Why don't we take a break from all this? I'd like to buy you dinner. Sort of a thank you for helping me with my problem. Then we'll come back here, you can finish your thing and I can go to Kinko's."

I considered her proposal and thought, What the hell? It's only one ad. In fact, I could probably finish it early in the morning if I could get my ass out of bed early enough. Go for it, girl. I told her I'd meet her downstairs in the lobby in five minutes.

I did a quick backup on my Syquest drive, then shut down, checked all the doors to make sure we were locked up and then I was outta there. When I got to the lobby, she was waiting. I noticed she had put fresh lipstick on and she must have refreshed her perfume. Then I looked at my hands and ruefully noticed the rubber cement residue on my fingers which was turning black, and the ink stains from every color marker imaginable. I was certainly an attractive sight. "If you don't mind, I'd like to run into the bathroom and wash all this gunk off before we go," I said, and ran back down the hall. I scrubbed with that horrible green liquid soap and managed to get most of the rubber cement off. The marker stains were gradually fading, so I looked a little less like a five year old's human doodle pad. I didn't have any perfume to apply, but I did put some lip gloss on and I was ready.

I know you're all just dying for me to get to the juicy

parts, so I'll be brief about the next series of events. We took her car and went to a trendy Mexican-Irish restaurant in the area. Luckily, there are a lot of good places to eat around where we work—we're out in the suburbs, and it didn't used to be so heavily populated with good eateries. Anyway, we had some nachos and several Dos Equis and soon the conversation flowed as well as the beer. We talked the usual work talk—she was a draftsman, so we had something in common—T-squares! And after the beat-around-the-bush talk we finally got down to some personal items and we both discovered that we were lesbians. That is, I already knew I was one and I am sure she knew she was one too. I just didn't know about her and vice versa. As we left the restaurant, I was thinking how nice it was to have a friend working in the same building with me.

Sitting in her car, I made one of those snap decisions that sometimes turn out wonderfully, but more often than not turn into disaster. I was very attracted to her and I devised a creative way of spending more time with her tonight. "Why don't we pick up your copying job and go to Kinko's together? They also have Macs that they rent by the hour. I could finish my ad there while you're waiting for the copies. Then we could go get some coffee and maybe talk a little while longer." And maybe I could coax her back to my place for some more coffee....

To my surprise, she agreed! She took me back to the office to get my car. Just before she got out of her car she said, "It'll take me about five minutes to get my stuff together. I'll be right down. She went inside and then I remembered—I had forgotten to turn off my laser printer. Quickly I bolted out of the car and went inside.

Her office door was open as I went down the hall. I called out a greeting, telling her where I was going and that I'd be right back. She didn't answer. Maybe she had to use the ladies room. I walked into my office. My surge protector is inconveniently located under my drafting table, so I had to get down on my hands and knees to turn off the strip. As I was doing so, her voice came from behind me, "You have a cute ass, you know." I bumped my head on the underside of the table while trying to get up. Ouch. Not the first time that's happened. Bumping my head, that is. I turned around and she drew closer to me, and her hand brushed mine gently. Hmmm, a sign? Was I supposed to respond? "I was admiring your derriere myself," I heard myself say. Well, we've both got some killer lines here. No matter how bad our lines were, they were working.

She ran her fingers up my arm and around my neck. "I like your drafting table. It's bigger than mine." Now here was a pick-up line if I ever heard one. Maybe we weren't going to Kinko's...yet.

I put my hands on her waist, pulled her in and our lips touched. Mmmm, she was soft. We stood locked in this position forever, it seemed, and then she leaned into me, pushing me back against the drafting table. At least the table was in a semi-upright position so I had something to lean against. Her hands traveled up my waist, touching me in all the right areas. I stopped her and said, "Why don't we dim the lights a bit?—it's too bright in here." I ran over to my desk and turned on the little halogen desk lamp, putting it on the low setting. Then I ran over to the office door and turned off the main fluorescent lights and—presto!—instant bedroom. But no music. She was of the same mind as I was, apparently, because she had already switched on my radio, scanning the stations until she found one not too obnoxious. And there we were…ready for action.

She came over to me and started unbuttoning my shirt, her hands sliding in and all over my skin. My hands were not exactly idle at this point—I was pulling her blouse out of her skirt, unzipping her skirt. Gradually the floor became strewn with clothing. She had on some very nice underclothes which felt silky and sensuous to the touch. I had a wonderful time taking them off her, kissing her soft body all over as I was stripping her.

We were both naked and looking for a place to get comfy. Then I remembered there was an old blanket in the supply closet. I retrieved the blanket and spread it on the floor but she said, "No, let's use your drafting table." I wrinkled my nose at this thought. It was dirty and had tape goo and ink stains and, I mean—yukkk. But if I tried to clean it with solvent, then the place would smell like solvent. "Okay, but let me at least put the blanket on it—it's awfully dirty."

So I cleared the table of the triangles, pens, and T-square, fiddled with the adjusters until it was horizontal, spread the blanket and then we went horizontal. She pulled me on top of her and, well, here goes. Long, deep kisses. Tongues: exploring, thrusting, playing inside, biting her soft lips gently. Fingers: roving, finding a soft nipple, playing, twisting until the nipple changes shape, hardening. Sounds: low moaning, small sighs. The sounds she was making were filling my ears, drowning out the semi-obnoxious radio. Her hands were moving all over me. The combination of me touching her and her touching me was sending me into orbit. By the sounds she made and the way she was writhing, I knew I was affecting her the same way.

She sat up all of a sudden and said, "I've got a few toys in my bag. Let's play." She got off the table and came back with her briefcase, from which she plucked a set of handcuffs and a very nice pink dildo with a gorgeous leather harness. This girl was truly amazing—she must have been a Girl Scout. Always prepared. I was half expecting to see a Swiss Army Knife and a tin canteen next. What else did she have in that briefcase?

"The handcuffs are funky—see this one, the catch is loose. Sometimes it closes and stays, but most of the time it's loose." So a half-pair of handcuffs? I'd have to be creative, which I relish. She lay down on the table again. My drafting table was proving to be very versatile, but one thing it doesn't have is a headboard. Aha! My architect's lamp. I tried sliding the handcuffs through the stem of the lamp. It was a tight fit, but after some shoving I got them through. I attached the one cuff that worked to her left hand, then attached the funky one to her right hand. The clasp wouldn't stay shut, so I called upon my innate creativity again and jury-rigged the cuff with some white artist's tape. I had masking tape, but this stuff is stronger. Plus it wouldn't hurt when I removed it.

So she was tied up, hands over her head, which is what she must have wanted. After looking at her lying there in bondage, nipples erect, I was even more turned on. I went back to playing with her breasts—they were small, tight, and lots of fun to play with. My other hand found her clit, which was very damp, and I worked on making her even wetter. The juice was flowing now. I massaged her clit slowly, my fingers teasing, and then as her sighs grew more intense and I could feel her rocking, I went a little faster and a little deeper. We had a nice rhythm going now, as though we had done this together for ages.

I wanted to taste her, so down I went. She was sweet and sticky—the honey pot was full. She spread her legs a bit more and I just moved in. I was hoping she'd push me in with her hands, but then I remembered her hands were cuffed over her head. Next time. But her legs were nice and strong and she gripped me with them, wrapping me in a vise from which I was in no hurry to get out of. My tongue took over for my fingers, going even faster and deeper, and she was starting to go into a deeper rhythm. She was going to come any second and from the way she was moving it seemed like it would be a big one. It was. She let out a yell that made me shudder, not from the sheer volume—it was LOUD—but from the force and the intensity—it was from deep within. She put her whole body into that one. I lay on top of her, happy and a little tired.

I might have fallen asleep right there when she kissed me and said, "We'd better go. Like it or not, I've still got to go to Kinko's and get this done before tomorrow." I rolled off her, turned the lights on and started to pick up my clothes, when she said, "Hey, how about a little help?" I looked at her, naked and bound to my lamp and said, "Well, this could cost you..." and then I quickly said, "Just kidding." I had no idea if her sense of humor was as sick as mine, so I didn't want to push it. I put on my bra, underwear and pants and then set out to free her.

"The key is in my wallet, in the change pouch." I searched her briefcase, found her wallet and drew the key out of the change pouch. I unlocked the good cuff, then I removed the drafting tape from the funky one, expecting the cuff to just fall apart as it had done initially. It didn't. I tried the key and it still wouldn't open. She looked at me in a panic, her eyes widening. "Can you slide your hand out of it?" I pleaded. She tried, but her hands were just a little too big. "Try to at least pull the handcuffs through the lamp so we can get you out of the lamp." They wouldn't budge. She was stuck, handcuffed inside my lamp. Frantically I tried to think if we had anything in the storage closet that resembled a saw, but I knew we didn't. We were stuck here.

No we weren't. The base of the lamp clips on to the table and is held by a screw vise. I slipped under the table, unplugged the lamp, unscrewed the base and the lamp was freed from the table. She was free, in a sense. One hand was in a handcuff attached to a lamp. But at least she was mobile. We needed a hacksaw and maybe some bolt cutters. I mentally reviewed my toolbox back at my apartment and my quick inventory search revealed a hacksaw. We would have to go shopping for bolt cutters if we needed them. An image appeared instantly of the two of us walking through Home Depot, her with a lamp hanging from her arm.

I looked at her with the lamp handcuffed to her arm and said, "You've got to admit, this could be a new look for you." Again my horrible sense of humor. But she stood there, naked in her new quasi-industrial look, and laughed. Then she hugged me and said, "Come on, genius, figure out how I'm gonna put my clothes on." A new challenge. I love challenges.

Her bra wasn't too difficult, and underwear went smoothly. I was trying to figure out how to get the sleeve of her blouse over the lamp when I heard something—someone else was in the building! A male voice boomed, "Anybody here?" Christ, it was my boss! What was he doing here at 10:00 at night? And from the sound of him, he was right at the Xerox room. Now we were in some deep, deep, deep trouble. How to explain this tidy little situation? He was getting closer.

I quickly threw my shirt on, looked at Karen in her

underwear and lamp and whispered, "Get under the table now." She had this look on her face that clearly indicated she thought I was out of my mind, but she crawled under the table as instructed. I threw the rest of her clothes in my bottom desk drawer, threw the blanket over her, sat down in my chair, wheeled the chair in front of the table and whispered, "No matter what happens, don't move or make a sound." There was no movement from the interesting shape under the blanket, so my message must have gotten through. Now I had to calm down and try to get him out of here.

He appeared in the doorway and said, "What's going on? How come you're still here?"

"Well, Don, you know I had meetings all day today and the ads were due for the Johnson account, so I had to get them done somehow."

"You've really been putting in a lot of extra time lately, haven't you?"

Yeah, if he only knew what my extra hours amounted to tonight… I nodded my head yes in response to his question. And then he did the unthinkable. He came into my office, pulled up an extra chair and sat down right in front of me. Suddenly I realized that my office didn't look like I had been working at all—the table was completely clear of all my tools, my computer and peripherals were shut off. It looked like I hadn't been here at all. I had to think fast.

"I just finished shutting everything down—I'm really exhausted, and I was getting ready to leave when you showed up," I lied, hoping he'd buy it. I prayed that his eyes wouldn't wander in the direction of my table. But he seemed focused on something else; I wasn't sure if he even heard what I said. And then he spoke:

"I didn't get a chance to see you today, and I was going to try and meet with you first thing tomorrow morning. But after seeing all the time you've put in tonight, I think you should take tomorrow off. Besides, all I was going to tell you was that Ron and I have been extremely pleased with the work you've done for us. Your attention to detail and willingness to go the extra mile to get the job done—this isn't just a job for you, it's something you live for and thrive on. So we've done some talking and we've decided it's time for you to move up. As of next Friday, you're our new Creative Director. That is, if you want the promotion."

He was smiling like the Cheshire Cat and he leaned over and shook my hand. Just as his hand slipped out of mine, a very muffled "achoo" came from beneath my table. Quickly I ran my hand across my nose and sniffed, saying, "Excuse me—think I might be catching a cold."

"Gezhundheit" he said. Then he got up and said, "Get the hell out of here and get some rest. Can't have you getting sick now. I'll make the announcement tomorrow. Welcome to management. You've earned it." Still grinning, he turned and walked out. I was frozen to the chair—I dared not move, lest he turn around again and see the results of my hard work under the drafting table. I whispered, "Stay right here. I'll be right back," and I tiptoed out to the hall to make sure he was gone. I walked down the hall and peered out the front window and saw his headlights flash, then fade as he made the turn out of the parking lot.

I went back into my office, where I discovered Karen had emerged from her cocoon. I glared at her. She was smiling as slyly as Don had been. "I'm sorry, my nose was itchy and I couldn't help it. Now, miss executive, what do we do about my lamp problem?"

A good executive would consider each issue carefully, then look at how each issue affects the whole picture. And then each issue would be dealt with accordingly. And now for my first attempt at the executive decision-making process:

Issue #1: I told Karen we would go to Kinko's and finish her copy job. "And don't worry—I'll take it inside so you don't have to bring your lamp into the store." Then we would drive back and leave the job in her office.

Issue #2: I told her to come back to my place, where I would saw the lamp and handcuffs off her arm.

Issue #3: We would spend the rest of the night making love, and probably all of tomorrow as well.

"And there's one more thing" I said, tenderly kissing her neck. "Yes, boss?" she sighed, wrapping her arms around me.

"We're going to get a pair of handcuffs that work."

Philadelphia, but I changed all that. At least I changed the way my house was. The neighborhood and Philadelphia—I can't quite change. But I'm working on it. Hey, one thing at a time. So anyway, I gutted the second floor, made it a loft, put the staircase in (the jury's still out on that improvement) and voila! Instant artist's loft. Which suits me fine. Because I am an artist. I gutted the downstairs and made it one big room—kitchen area, steel support poles where bearing walls used to be—but then the rest is my studio. I like to work big and it's no problem with the extra ceiling space. Furniture I don't concern myself with—it's only gonna get paint on it anyway. I have milk crates downstairs for guests. Besides, I consider the upstairs my real living area. I did all the work myself, with some help from a few fag friends for the drywall and joist removal. The upstairs is pretty nice—my bedroom plus a second bedroom, a room which could be a third bedroom but which I use as my library. I have so many books and nowhere to put them. There's one bathroom upstairs and a powder room downstairs. The upstairs bath is cool—leg tub, shower ring, old style tile—those little white rectangles with hardly any grout in-between—and old style fixtures. So, that's my house. Now, where were we?

Ah yes, I had just glided down the stairs and was about to grind some coffee. What time was it? 9 A.M. Too early for a Sunday. But I had some serious work to do today. I had a commission coming today—some woman was coming over to discuss a mural for her house. It could be good money. She was from Lower Merion, a rather ritzy suburb of Philadelphia. I hadn't seen her house—she was bringing pictures with her—but knowing Lower Merion fairly well and being familiar with her street I knew the typical house on her street was a large three story white mini-mansion with a circular driveway, lots of trees, and exquisite woodwork throughout. I'll bet there were at least three fireplaces with ornate mantles, lots of authentic Oriental carpet, and a garage filled with Beamers or Lincolns or whatever they happened to be into at the moment. Anyway, she probably had money and was willing to spend it if the product was good. I was determined to make sure I had my best stuff available.

So I showered, ran a comb through my buzz-cut, moussed up, and clothed myself in my best Georgia O'Keefe black. Then I started inventory. I had some interesting pieces on the wall, but there were other things I had had to collect from various clients. I had them lined up on the far wall, ready for viewing. I could do just about anything—pen & ink, charcoal, pencil, oil, acrylic—and I had examples of everything. She was really vague on the phone—she said she had seen me at a local artists exhibition in Rittenhouse Square last summer, and she liked my work—but she didn't say what it was she liked or what medium she liked or anything. She wouldn't even say her last name. At this point I didn't care—she had money to blow and she wanted me—or my work, that is. And I needed money. There was a mortgage to pay, after all.

The buzzer rang at ten o'clock. She was punctual. I opened the door and I saw her. I nearly fell backwards. She was beautiful. Blonde hair swept up in a bun, tall, thin, angular. Definitely Main Line horse set. She probably had horses at Devon every year. I introduced myself. Her name was Corinna. Last name I can't repeat, because those of you from the Philly area will recognize it. Suffice it to say, I had seen her name in the society pages. She was a blue blood. She could definitely pay my mortgage for a year, if the price was right. And if I was good enough.

"Come on in—sorry the place is a mess, but this is what it is," I heard myself say. What a dope. Couldn't think of anything more imaginative than that?

"It's okay—I like an artist's place. It's a creative place."

I heard something in her voice—couldn't put my finger on it. Well, better get moving.

"Want some coffee? It's freshly ground."

"No, I've had my allotment for the day."

"Wish I could say the same," I muttered while I poured another cup. Just to be polite, I thought. I really didn't need any more caffeine. I just thought I would make it look as though I wasn't really awake yet. Though her entrance definitely woke me up. "Have a look around. See if anything moves you."

"Thanks. I will." She walked around, hands entwined behind her back.

I was barely able to contain myself, nervously drinking my coffee. I couldn't get over her looks. She was absolutely stunning. In my entire miserable little dyke life I had never seen a woman like her. Her jacket had to cost at least five hundred dollars. I was accustomed to scouring my beat-up Toyota for any hidden change just to buy cigarettes. I decided not to focus on my money problems, but rather on something a bit more pleasant. Her. And so I continued to watch her as she browsed my studio. She stopped in front of each piece, lingering. Sometimes she cocked her head as if she had not heard something the painting had said to her. I continued to sip my coffee, thinking nasty little thoughts about what we might do later when she was finished browsing. God, was I awful. I desperately needed to do something about my life. Like get one. I was not dealing well with being single and uninterested.

"I want to show you some pictures of the room in the house where I want the mural," she said. "Could we sit down somewhere?"

I looked around my suddenly horrible studio and realized that we'd have to sit on milk crates. "As you can see, I don't have any real furniture down here—it's more of a studio. If you like, we could go upstairs. I have a library up there with some couches. It might be more comfortable." I walked over to her—what was her perfume? I thought it intoxicating—and directed her toward the stairs.

"A spiral staircase. How charming."

"They're charming, but they can be deadly if you're not careful. I know. I've fallen a few times."

"Really? What happened?"

I was too embarrassed to admit that I'd been a little drunk and had had lovers over, so I just fudged a bit with, "Well, if you don't have rubber soles on your shoes, you're out of luck."

She laughed and looked down at her expensive heels and said, "I guess I'd better remove these." Which she did. Then she started up the stairs.

"Hold on to the rail," I called behind her. And what a behind it was. I was beside myself. If I don't chill out I'm gonna blow the whole thing. Got to get a grip.

We made it to the top. I moved in front of her and showed her to the library. I wasn't lying—I did have a small couch, table and an old but comfy chair. I sat on the couch; she on the chair. She opened up her purse and brought an envelope out. I leaned over to look at the photos. She was talking about one of the pictures. I couldn't quite see what she was talking about, so I got up and walked over behind the chair. I looked down at the picture, but I didn't see the photo. I only saw breasts. She did not have a bra on, and when I leaned a little farther in I could see everything—nipples, the fullness of her breasts. Her nipples were erect, which excited me even more. I had to move—if I didn't, there would be trouble.

She turned around to face me and said, "I suppose it's hard to get the true feeling from just photos. Maybe you should come over to the house and see it for yourself."

I agreed, and said, "I guess that means that you like what you've seen."

Corinna said, "I wouldn't say yes, definitely, but I'm inclined toward your work, if that's what you're driving at."

Well, it wasn't a ringing endorsement, but it was the best news I'd heard in a while. So we made plans to meet the next day at 10:00 at her house. I prayed she wouldn't change her mind in the next twenty four hours.

Well, the time of the appointment arrived and so did I. I maneuvered my trusty Toyota down the snow-covered streets of Lower Merion (didn't the rich have any snow plows?) until I arrived in the vicinity of her house. Her castle, that was more like it. I pulled into the circular drive—wasn't I right?—and parked my little rusty banged up chariot next to the Mercedes 350 SEL and the Lexus. I was way out of my league. I just hoped my artwork was in her league. I negotiated the brick walkway and stood under the front entrance way, ringing the bell. The door opened—it wasn't her! A tall, silver-haired distinguished looking gentleman was behind the door. "May I help you?" I stated my name and my purpose. "Oh yes, my wife is expecting you." Wife? Well, I knew she had to be married, I just wasn't prepared for grandpa. But I guess that's how it happens in this world.

Grandpa showed me in. I waited in the foyer (or lobby, it was big enough) and nervously paced, looking at the walls, trying to see what they were into. Fortunately they were very astute. They liked naive artists from Pippin and Rousseau (prints only!) to Winslow Homer, to Pollock prints and so forth. I wondered why she wanted me for the mural. "Excuse me, my wife will be down in a minute. I have business to attend to, so I'll be leaving. Please make yourself at home," Grandpa said. He turned and left. I walked out of the foyer into the living room, and sat on the nearest chair. I heard the sound of an engine, then the sound of tires on macadam growing ever so distant.

My legs were shaking. Maybe I should leave. I felt very uncomfortable and was thinking about how I would phrase my exit speech when a hand on my shoulder startled me. I flinched, turned around and it was her! I looked down at my shoulder and saw her hand frozen there. Such neatly manicured nails. I bite mine. And long fingers (if she played the piano, maybe she would play me!), and I said, stupidly, "Well, here I am. Prompt as always."

She replied, "I expected nothing less. I'm a busy woman. I have many things that claim my attention. We'd better get started."

I wanted to crawl in a hole. I was so outclassed. Maybe I'd better just pack up my ball and go home. This wasn't fun anymore.

We stood at the bottom of the stairs—a circular stairway, all hardwood, with a wonderful wood rail and banisters. She said: "The room I want the mural in is on the third floor. But I want to show you the rest of the house. You don't mind, do you?"

"I would love to see your house." I was beginning to enjoy myself, getting lost in the tour. Big, wide crown moldings on the ceilings, magnificent hardwoods, the kitchen fabulous with a Jenn-Air island, Italian tile on the floor and countertops—I was in designer heaven. We walked through the smaller bedrooms, each with their own bath (I never had my own bath when I was growing up), and then we arrived at the master bedroom. Or suite. It was a combination of several rooms—bedroom, sitting room, dressing room, his and her bathrooms. She directed me towards the sitting room, where there was a sofa and love seat. She sat down on the sofa and patted the area next to her and motioned me to join her, which I did.

"So, tell me about yourself," she said.

"What do you mean?" I asked.

"I want to know where you've been, where you grew up, went to school, who your influences are," she said.

So I told her. I don't know why, but I found myself telling her everything, including the names of my parents, my dog's name when I grew up, the first drawing I made. I stopped when I got to the present. I figured she knew everything she needed to know.

But then she threw me a curve: "Are you married?"

Why was she interested in that? I was having a hard enough time keeping my wits together around her just because she was so beautiful. I figured, well I'll just go for the gold. Maybe I'll lose the job. Maybe not. So I told her, "I'm into women, frankly."

"I thought so."

Ah, she knew. Well, now that this was over maybe we could move on to discussing the job. So I started to get up, but she put her hand on my arm and said: "Don't. Stay."

I slowly sat down, looking at her face. It was divine. She had a curious smile. I found my gaze traveling down her body, away from her face. She had a white blouse on, covered by a sweater vest, but even through the vest I could see her nipples protrude. She is either very cold or very horny, I thought. I didn't think her house was all that cold, even though it was a big old house.

She moved toward me. "My husband met you at the door. We have been married ten years. He is fifteen years older than me..." (which would have made her about forty-five, I guessed) "...and in the ten years we have been married I have never once had an orgasm. Not once. Do you understand me?"

I nodded my head, my mind scrambling to process this new and exciting information.

She continued: "We are not faithful to each other—he travels with his business and he says it's impossible for him. I have had my little affairs when the time has been right, and they have been enough. But not enough to bring me to my knees. Not enough to bring me complete satisfaction. Do you understand?"

Again, I nodded my head, completely entranced by

her story. I was unaware that my right hand was gripping my thigh, though I would see the bruises later.

"Do you find me attractive?" she said.

I was ready to choke. Be honest, I told myself. "I must confess, I've never seen a woman as beautiful as you are. I find you exquisite. Everything about you—your hands, your face, the way you walk, the way you smell—I know this sounds horribly crass, but I find myself thinking of making love to you." God, what had I done? I was just being honest, I told myself, but Geeez, did I have to put myself in jail? I guess I'd better get ready to leave—no way was I getting this job. No way was I coming back here at all. I was too ashamed to look at her, so I looked out the window. I should get up now. I said to her, "It's probably time I left. I don't think I should be here…." And then her hand was on my arm and I turned around to face her.

She looked at me for what seemed like a week, and then she said: "Make love to me, then. I want to feel what it's like to be made love to by a woman."

Gulp. She wanted me. ME. Now what do I do? I had made love to—well, probably at least fifty women and never had I felt so incompetent.

I said to her: "Why do you want a woman to make love to you? What could I give you that a man couldn't?" knowing perfectly well that I thought lesbian sex far superior to hetero sex, but I wasn't going to tell her that. I wanted to hear it from her.

She moved closer and said: "I think women are

softer. I think women care very deeply. I think women are more sensuous. But that's what I think. Show me. Show me that I'm right."

Well, the gauntlet has been thrown. I had to answer.

I reached for her. I held her face in both hands, caressing her eyelids, her nose, tracing the outline of her lips. I kissed her. Her lips were dry, a little chapped. Too much time outdoors at the horse track, I thought. But the more I kissed her lips, the softer they got as the wetness from mine mixed with hers. Her fingers gripped my shoulders. I kissed her lips, down her neck, behind her ears (I hadn't realized how attractive her ears were), I moved inside her collar. My hands started loosening her buttons; my fingers slid inside her shirt and found soft skin. She moaned a little, I think. Maybe it was me. I could feel my own wetness. I moved my hand down the outside of her shirt until I had her nipples between my fingers. I wanted the real thing, so I quickly pulled her sweater vest over her head. She was very cooperative. I unfastened the remaining buttons and spread her shirt apart until I could see her breasts, free from their confines. I placed both hands on them, slowly moving around, grasping her nipples between my fingers and gently massaging them, making them harder, more erect. I wanted to taste them. I bent down and put my lips to her breast, circling the nipple with my tongue, sucking, playing. A moan—it was her, not me.

She took my hand. We rose from the couch and walked from the sitting room into the master bedroom.

She lay down on the bed. I lay down on top of her, my face nestled in her breasts. My hands moved down to her tailored slacks. I found the buttons—buttons, no zipper. I would need two hands. I sat up and started unbuttoning. As I unbuttoned, she said, "Kiss me as you unbutton me." I leaned down and kissed her navel, her hips, her thighs. I pulled her pants down and pulled at her underwear, kissing her all the time. Her skin was smooth and smelled good, expensive. I wondered what it would be like to take a shower with her. I had her underwear down and I had her cunt in front of me. I raised my hand and stroked her hair—it was soft. I ran my fingers between her legs and felt soft, sticky wetness. My hand trailed down her leg, hot sticky wetness leaving its trail. I wanted her to know how wet she was. I started to ask her if she had ever been this wet before, but she beat me and said: "You make me feel so good. I've never felt this hot before. Please, please fuck me now."

What was I to do? I wanted to eat her, but she wanted fucking. Maybe she would like both. I put my fingers into her cunt; it was so slippery, wet, sticky. I slowly moved my hand in and out, in and out. She moaned and moved her body in rhythm with me. I moved my head down and tasted her. Salty, sweet wetness. The nectar of life. My tongue moved across her clit, which was very erect, back and forth, the wetness flowing. At the same time my fingers pumped in and out. Tongue and fingers, in and out, back and forth. Her moans were louder, more intense. I was becoming very aroused. I kept it up, she began to shake, her legs twitching, her hips moving in spasms. Her wetness was sliding down her thighs, all over me, my face. I was bathing in her come.

She reached for me and grasped my shoulder with one hand, gripping me so hard I thought I would bleed from her fingernails. I kept going, in and out, back and forth, until finally she pushed into me in one final arc, her body shaking, legs uncontrollable, and then she let out a scream unlike any I've ever heard. I was afraid someone would hear, and I sat up, looking around. She pulled me down to her and sighed, "No one's here. Just lie here. Stay with me."

I did as I was told, my face on her breast. I kissed her breasts, touched her everywhere. She was incredible. I had never experienced anyone coming that violently. She looked at me and said, "Now I know what it's all about." I asked her if it was okay and she said, "I've just had the most unbelievable experience and you want to know if it was okay." I felt like I was the most important person in the world.

I heard a muffled noise from somewhere on the first floor. I sat up abruptly, nervously looking around. She lay there, unconcerned.

"What's that?" I asked.

She said, "Probably the maid. She won't come up here. Lie down."

But my mood was disrupted. It was clear to me that I

just couldn't go back. So I got up, walked around a bit and waited for her.

She arose, put her blouse and pants back on and said: "We haven't talked about your painting. I want to show you where you'll be working."

She led me to the third floor, showed me the wall where she wanted the mural.

I said to her, "But the third floor, it's kind of isolated, isn't it? I mean, no one will see this mural."

She looked at me with a smile and said: "Precisely. It's only for me. I want you to paint what happened today. In your own way. What happened to you and what happened to me. This is my room. No one comes in here but me. And now you, since you'll be working here."

"When do you want me to start?"

"Right away. Tomorrow okay?"

"Tomorrow's fine. Will you be here?"

"Of course. I'll have lunch for you. You'll need a break every now and then. You can spend the night if you want."

"Will your husband be here?"

"No, he's away. But don't get any ideas. No one sleeps in this bed with me but him."

I instantly turned away. Oh well. At least I had a job. But I felt her hand on my shoulder and I turned around to face her and I heard her say:

"Not in this bed, but there are eight other beds that we haven't slept in."

I looked into her china blue eyes, kissed her on the lips, let her taste herself on my lips, and I heard myself ask if I could bring my cat. After all, Georges would not tolerate being left out.

I Paint the Mural, Georges Catches the Mice

We've all got our little jobs to do in this life. Some of us make out better than others, that's for sure. If you read our first adventure, "Still Life," then you know that I was about to be gainfully employed painting a mural on a third floor wall in a big old house on the Main Line owned by Corrina, a stunningly beautiful, married, slightly older woman. And you also know that Corrina, the lady of the house, had an incredible orgasm when I made love to her the day I came over to her house. So then you probably know that she asked us—me and Georges, my cat—to move in with her while I painted the mural.

Don't get me wrong—at first I was absolutely in love with the idea of me living the hoity toity life on the Main Line. For a while, it was like a fairy tale—every morning waking up with Georges on my head in a big puffy bed. Having a maid do my laundry. Driving the Mercedes while taking Corrina shopping (she hated to drive). I only used my banged up Toyota when I needed to go in town to get supplies. Corrina would have had a fit if I ever took her Mercedes into Philadelphia. ("The way they drive down there? Like animals.") Coming home, pulling into the circular drive like I owned the place. And the nights... Corrina's husband hadn't been around since I arrived. He was away on a three month business trip to China. He was in the import/export business, so Corrina had said. Well, needless to say, he just exported himself out of the picture and Corrina imported me in. And what a picture we made.

We went to see the Philadelphia Orchestra regularly and had box seats at the Academy. Sometimes we would attend a charity event, and the next day I would see Corrina's name in the Inquirer society pages. No mention of me, however. "It's extremely important for me to keep up appearances. If anyone in my social circle found out I was having a lesbian affair, it would be the end of me." The gospel according to Corrina.

So, wherever we went, Corrina always had me walk three steps behind her, and not to mingle with her more than two times during the event. If anyone ever asked who I was, I always told them my name and that I was an artist. If anyone asked me if I knew Corrina, I always said, "Yes, I'm doing a painting for her," and that was the end of it. The only time we were together was when we went to see the orchestra and didn't use the box seats. Corrina also had two seats next to each other in the back row, where we could sit and hold hands and just let the music take us away.

Corrina hated my smoking, so I promised her I'd stop, and I did for a while. Lately, I'd just been sneaking a couple outside while I take a break from my painting. I must admit I felt better. And I looked better too, now that I'd been working out. The entire basement area in Corrina's house had been converted into a home gym, with Nautilus, steppers, bikes, free weights. So I'd been working out a lot, and enjoying the results in the full length mirrors.

Corrina enjoyed the results too. The woman was forty-five and she's a sex maniac. Every night we did it, it seemed. I didn't think the day would come when I would refuse sex, but lately I've been trying to drop some hints ("I really must have overdone it on the turpentine today, I've got such a headache." Or: "I think I killed my arms with the weights—could we maybe try tomorrow?")

But the pay was nice. Corrina and I agreed on a fee of $20,000 for the painting, and every week she wrote me a check for $500, the balance to be paid upon completion. So far, I'd collected, let's see, two weeks in January, it was now the beginning of May and…wow, $7,000. I was able to pay my mortgage 6 months in advance, pay off almost half of my bills, and keep Georges in cat food for the rest of the year. Georges had had a banner time with the mice, too. Apparently, the mice in the suburbs are much tastier than the ones in the city, or so he said when we butted heads and had our morning chat before breakfast. "Another thirteen grand and you'll be swimming in gourmet mice," I told him, if I ever got the damn mural finished. I'd been so busy running around with Corrina, or doing errands for her that it'd been almost two weeks since I'd touched a brush. And I wasn't even halfway through.

Living there in blissful straight suburbia had put me a bit out of touch with my old dyke-style (short for dyke lifestyle). Hardly seen any of my friends since I'd been at Corrina's. I was never at my house except to pick up mail—I brought all my plants with me to Corrina's so they wouldn't be neglected. My answering machine calls I could pick up by remote, though there hadn't been very many these days.

Late Sunday afternoon I stood in my studio, shuffling through the mail. Corrina was out riding, which was odd for a Sunday. But she didn't like coming over to my place anyway, so it was a good excuse to get out of coming with me. Give the Toyota a run and clean out the carb. Standing in my very empty studio, I looked around and all of a sudden I felt like crying. I really missed the old place, with the paint splatter marks on the floor and walls. I walked over to the spiral staircase and ran my hand down the black rail. Just as I was about to be overcome by a completely disgusting wave of nostalgia, the phone rang. I rushed over to pick it up before the machine could, breathlessly mumbling, "Hello."

"Hey, babe, is that really you?" It was Judy, my third ex (Marge was my first ex, Janet was my second).

"Jude, long time no talky. How the hell are you?" I hadn't seen Judy in almost a year. She lived in Northeast Philly, and talked like it.

"I was thinking, you know, maybe we could get together and have a brewski. I hear you been outta circulation a little. We could do some catching up. Listen, I'm headed downtown in about an hour. Whyntcha meet me at the Dyke Stop?"

The Dyke Stop was, as you've probably guessed, the local dyke hangout, down on Twelfth and Chestnut Streets. Its male counterpart, the Bike Stop, was just around the corner. In my current state of woo-woo, it took me all of two seconds to decide that I really did miss seeing my old friends, and yes I'd be there in about an hour. I hung up the phone, thinking of Judy. She talked crude but, boy she looked good, or had looked good when I last saw her. And Judy could make love, that's for sure. Not that Corrina couldn't. I was sure she could. I just couldn't get her to do it to me. In all this time, I was not able to get her to make love to me. "I'm just not ready to try it," she'd say. "Give me a little more time. I know I'll be able to do it someday." And so on we went, me the dutiful gigolo, keeping my straight girl-friend happy while she kept me in dough, kept me around, kept me so busy I never had time for my friends…in other words, I was being kept.

The more I thought about my current situation, the more morose I got. Happy Hour couldn't have come soon enough. I parked illegally on the street—if they towed the Toyota away, no big loss. After all, I was a kept woman. I had a Mercedes now. I walked over to the entrance, opened the big industrial steel black door and stepped inside. Home. This is what it felt like. When was the last time I was here? Had to be…hmmm, New Year's Eve. Almost five months ago. Stepping inside the dark bar from the brightness of the outdoors made my eyes go wacko for a few moments until I could adjust to the light. Still squinting from the contrast, I looked around the bar and then I saw a hand waving. It was Judy, at the far end of the bar.

I walked over, she stood up and we hugged and kissed on the cheek. "Damn, you look great. What'dya lose weight or something?" Judy gushed. I told her I'd been working out a couple of days a week. "It shows, that's for sure," she said, her lips curving upward in approval.

"And you look like someone I'd love to go out with," I said, eyeing her up and down. She did look pretty spectacular—tight black jeans tucked into biker boots, black leather jacket, long brown-black hair cascading in ringlets down her shoulders.

"You used that line on me a dozen times before we broke up," she replied. "Whaddaya want—another go-round?"

I laughed and said, "What I'd really like is a big glass of beer. Let's go sit down."

We sat at the bar. Judy motioned for the bartender to bring me a bottle of Beck's Dark, which I immediately poured into the glass, the creamy head foaming, and raised the glass to my lips. The bitter dark liquid flowed over my taste buds, the foam making a little mustache on my upper lip, which Judy laughingly wiped away with a bar napkin. I swallowed slowly, savoring the taste and remembering that the last time I'd had a Beck's Dark was the night before I met Corrina. I hadn't had any beer since then. Corrina didn't drink much, and the only thing she did drink was wine—good wine, which she had plenty of. And that's all I had been drinking, until now. I felt like I had been away in a foreign country.

"So tell me, what's been goin' on witchyou. How come you ain't been around?" Judy said, sipping her Coors Light.

And I told her the whole story. With each new revelation, her eyes widened and she seemed fascinated with minutiae ("I always wanted to know this: do they really wear those funny little glasses on their noses at the opera?" "When you're at the horse show, why is it some people wear little red jackets and some people wear little black jackets?" "You have your own bathroom? Wow.") And on and on. When I was finished, I took a long swig of my beer and said, "So you think I'm an idiot, right?"

She looked at me and said, "Whatever makes you happy, hon. If you like this straight chick and she treats you right, then go for it. But it don't sound like you're being treated the way you should be. I mean, you may as well be invisible. You can't acknowledge your relationship, you gotta walk three steps behind her in public. And that sex stuff…she might have a great bod and all, but when is she gonna do you? I can't imagine sleeping witchyou and not making love to you." And Judy ran her hand up my arm as she looked longingly at me.

Whose idea was this, to break up? It had been mine, of course. Me, the artist, the one with the "edge-acation," as Judy liked to put it. What had I not liked about her? The way she talked? Her lack of education? (Judy had quit school in the 11th grade after her father had died, and she went to work as a dancer in one of the sleaze bars downtown.) Judy's language skills might not win her the silver-tongued orator award, but she could cut right to the point. And she was very attractive, not in the exquisite, fine-china way of Corrina. Judy was downright hot looking, especially in the outfit she had on right now. As I began to feel the beer, I suddenly realized that the ache between my legs was not me having to empty my bladder—I was hot for Judy. Hot for her to do me.

I reached for her hand across the bar, our fingers weaving together. "So, you seeing anyone, Jude? What's going on with you? Still have the plant shop?" Judy and her sister Natalie owned a flower shop, Judy having long ago given up dancing in bars for something a little less lucrative but a little safer. And Judy filled me in on her life—yeah, she was seeing someone, but it wasn't a commitment thing. As usual I wasn't listening very closely. I was busy squeezing her hand while she gently but firmly stroked my thigh, making the ache between my legs a sharp pain.

"Ow," I said.

"What?"

"Nothing."

"You can't fool me. Maybe you can fool your little Main Line girl, butchya can't fool Jude. Jude knows when you're hot. Wanna get outta here? Why don't we go back to your place for a while?"

I looked at her in her black leather oozing with heat, and I thought—What the hell? And so we went outside. Amazingly, my Toyota was still there, illegally parked and with no ticket. A sign, perhaps?—my life might be headed for a change. I have always hated change. It usually means bad things. Nothing good ever happens with change. Maybe this time the outcome would be different. I decided to just go with it and worry about the consequences later.

We barely got through my front door—we were all over each other, Judy's tongue on mine, my hands on her breasts. Her hands were already inside my jeans, the zipper having achieved casualty status way back in the car. I was pleasantly buzzed from the beer, and very much into what was going on. Life in straight suburbia had its advantages, but I was jonesing for my old dyke-style and I was getting a badly needed fix. Judy, the pusher-woman, was giving it to me and good. She had me on the floor, my pants were around my ankles and my underwear soon followed via a violent tearing-away motion by Judy. I protested that my boots were still on and couldn't we take them off along with my pants, but Judy wouldn't hear of it, so I was left bound at the ankles by my clothing. Not to worry—Judy had other distractions planned so that I wouldn't think about my bondage.

She stripped off her shirt and pants—God I had forgotten how wonderful she looked, all sinewy and sleek—and she lay down on top of me, slowly rubbing her pussy against mine. If I had had a dick, it would have been taller than Billy Penn's hat, I was so aroused by now. I felt wetness seep out of me. She rubbed her nipples against mine, then started sucking me, her tongue jabbing at my nipple, then her lips closing in and pulling. One nipple, then the other. Back and forth, all the while she kept rubbing against my clit. I was going through the roof big-time, and she knew it. "You want me, baby, I knew it. All this time away and we still got it. Come on, baby, put it in my face. Give Jude your pussy and I'll take care of the rest."

Judy couldn't speak a word of English without Philla-u-faying-it up, but she could talk sex talk, that's for sure. I wasn't about to argue with her either. I arched up and gave it to her, what she asked for. And I got more than I had gotten in the last year—she dove into me like an Arab in the Sahara Desert without water for three months suddenly coming upon an oasis. She played with me at first, her tongue teasing my clit, but then she just nose-dived (tongue first), lapping at me, then she was in me, it seemed. Her tongue going in and out and all around, she was devouring me. My eyes were closed and I just got lost, feeling everything, trying to savor each touch, each taste like I was having an expensive dinner that I might not have again. Dessert was coming. Or rather, I was. All the pent up emotion of the last five months literally poured out of me—the agony and ecstasy of Corrina—and I just exploded into Judy's mouth, my body shaking and pulsing even after I knew I had spent my wad.

We lay together on the floor for a few minutes, Judy caressing my head and I just a limp rag doll. I'm not sure when we fell asleep, but when I woke it was after 7:00. Oh, no, Corrina would be having a fit right about now. Quickly I got up and started to put myself back together. Judy sat on the floor and said, "You an' me, we're good together. Face it, you miss everything—not just me but your life. You have no life right now that's yours. Everything is Corrina this, Corrina that. You oughtta hurry up, finish that painting and get the hell outta there. Come back home where you belong. I'll be waitin' for ya."

Her words ricocheted around inside my head as I drove back to Lower Merion. Of course, she was right about everything. Here I was, Little Miss Sex Slave to the Great Straight White Mistress. Where was this all getting me? Sure it was a big commission and a steady paycheck, but I could've had five paintings done by now. And I was getting lazy—hadn't painted in two weeks. If I was nothing else, I was disciplined when it came to my work—I always, always painted every day, whether I felt like it or not. I had let myself get totally swept up in "recruiting" a beautiful straight chick into the lesbian life, yet I couldn't get her to make love to me. She loved me in her bed and in her house, but I was a stranger in public. It was time to end the grand experiment. I pulled into the drive, cut the motor and went inside. As the door closed behind me in the vestibule, I heard swift, strident footsteps. Corrina. And she was pissed.

"I have been worried sick. Where have you been?" she slowly spoke in measured tones that, while giving the outward appearance of calm, were a clear indication to me of her anger. Corrina never raised her voice except when she was laughing. When she got angry, she got quieter and more determined sounding.

"I had to stop at my house and pick up mail. I told you that. While I was there, an old friend called whom I haven't seen in a year, so we met downtown and had a couple of beers. I'm sorry I didn't call; I know I should have." God this was disgusting. I felt like a seven year old.

"You've been out drinking? You don't do that sort of thing. When did you start drinking beer?"

"About ten years ago, Corrina. I stopped when I moved in here. I guess I was trying to please you, knowing that you don't like to drink very much. But I don't think this is doing either of us any good. I think it's time we went our separate ways. I'll get the mural finished in two weeks, and then I'll be gone." Whew. I had done it. But it wasn't over yet. She stood, fuming silently. "What do you mean, go our separate ways? Haven't I given you everything?"

I looked at her, still beautiful in her anger, and said: "Corrina, this has been an experience I will never forget. But I think it's outlived its usefulness. You have to realize what this has been like for me. I've always been open about my sexuality. I've never had to hide. And now that's exactly what I'm doing. We can't ever be seen in public together—you wouldn't have it, you have an image to uphold. It makes it hard to enjoy those times because we aren't really together. "I feel like I've lost the person who used to be me. Today when I was out with Judy, I realized how far away from my lifestyle I've strayed. I can't draw a parallel for you except to think that if you'd stayed away from your friends for four months, weren't actively riding, didn't do any of the social things you used to do—then maybe you'd understand how I feel and maybe you could see my misery." I didn't say anything about making love to me—I was saving that for later, if I needed it.

She looked at me, her anger softening somewhat. "I didn't realize you were that unhappy. Why didn't you say something?"

"I tried to but it never seemed to be the right moment to bring it up." Something in her voice, in the way she was looking at me was making me lose my conviction, and I didn't know why but I felt very vulnerable.

"I don't want you to go. I've wanted to talk to you all day, but didn't know what to say. That's why I went riding, to think things out. I got a call today from Harry." Harry was her husband. "He wants to divorce me. I asked him why and he said that he'd heard through sources that I was having an affair. Which is ridiculous because we've always had affairs, so at first I was puzzled by his tactic. Then he went on, saying that he'd always been open and honest and he'd expected nothing less from me. Which is when I realized that the affair he was talking about was you. I haven't told him about you. That's one of the reasons I wanted this whole thing to be a secret. One of Harry's little fantasies when we were first married was to watch me make love with another woman. I refused to do so. Not because I was disgusted by the idea, but because I was afraid of how I might react. Even back then, I imagined that I might like it, as you've found out by now.

"So all this time Harry thinks the idea of being with another woman repulses me. And now he's found out about you, and naturally he's angry with me for not being straight with him." And Corrina started laughing.

"What's so funny?" I demanded.

And she said, "I just made a joke. Straight with him. Get it?"

And I did get it and started to chuckle a little. Corrina, maybe she's not so bad after all. This story was starting to develop an interesting little twist....

"And so Harry wants a divorce and I've had to think all day. I'll have to give up almost everything, you know. Part of the terms. Of course I'll get to keep the Mercedes, my horses, whatever else, like clothes, and I'll get a decent cash settlement—maybe two hundred fifty thousand. I'll probably have to board the horses. Harry gets this house and our vacation house in Sea Isle. Considering what's going on, I don't think you should continue with the mural." And she saw my crestfallen face. "I know you need the money and I'll make it up to you. Not now because I need every cent I can get my hands on until the settlement goes through. But it will be a quick settlement—Harry never likes to let things drag on. And then I'll also have some stock and interest payments due which will help."

And then Corrina moved a little closer to me, her voice softer and her hands on my hips, moving up slowly towards my upper body. "I think I'm ready to begin to learn how to live your life, to do the things you want to do, to have you teach me how. That is, if you still want me. When I got back from riding, I was ready to tell you to take me to your place and we could spend the night. We could still go, if you want to."

"Corrina, what would a nice girl like you want with my life?" I heard myself say. "There are people who hate people like me, you know. Just like people hate black people and Jews and Chinese people. And I refuse to hide anymore because the only way we can educate the rest of the world is to be out and show people that their prejudices are wrong. You'll have to be willing to be out too, if you want to be with me. Trying on a lifestyle is not as easy as trying on clothes. But if you're willing…" And I found myself softening up even more. "…then I am, too."

Corrina kept moving her hands on my body and said, "I love you. I've said it before in my life, but I'm not sure I really meant it. Until now."

And then the guilt set in. Guilt for Judy, for the afternoon of making love. I thought for an instant that I should tell her about Judy, then I decided that some things are better left unsaid. But then I completely lost my mind and said, "I didn't just have drinks with my old friend today, Corrina."

Corrina said, "I still love you."

"I love you Corrina. I've been in love with you since the day I saw you. Let's go back to my place and see if we can make it up the spiral stairs before I remove all of your clothes."

She smiled, kissed me on the lips (very forward for her) and said, "Let's see if we make it before I remove all of your clothes. And let's take the Mercedes, shall we? I think it's time she had her maiden voyage into town."

Let's Do It On-Line!

Turn computer on...booting up. Modem blinking its way through setup. Move the mouse and double click on icon...enter the password, dialing, connecting, checking network information, checking password... you're on-line. Let's see...browse through the departments. Ahh, People Connection. Gay & Lesbian Room. Let's go into this room and see who's there... Instant Message From RU Ready. RU Ready: I am. R U? Naked2: very very very. RU Ready: super very Naked2: Good. Good again (very very very). Naked2: Super very...all right, enough of this very stuff. Let's get down to business…RU Ready: what do you want to do/say? Naked2: Oh, I don't know, let's see…hmmm, what are you wearing, for starters? RU Ready: nothing Naked2: that was easy… RU Ready: sorry to be so boring… Naked2: Yes, that is pretty easy. I'm in boxer shorts and a robe RU Ready: does the robe feel good against your skin? RU Ready: I bet it's terry RU Ready: green RU Ready: boxers are red plaid RU Ready: you have brown hair Naked2: Not really. It's an old terry-cloth robe. I guess I should just take it off. No, maroon. Hey, maybe we could go to a private room…I have one. Boxers are not red plaid, they're white with little blue & red dots RU Ready: closely cropped pubic hair RU Ready: I said terry—got the colors wrong! Sounds good…I like you! Naked2: And I do have brown hair, dark brown almost black, and it's short (like Kevin Costner in the Bodyguard—an ugly hair cut, actually). Yes, closely cropped pubic hair. I know yours is. Let's see…are you blond? RU Ready: yes Naked2: It happens every time to me…blonds. Your head hair, is it longish? Longer than mine? RU Ready: shoulder Naked2: I suspected… And let's see, how tall are you? Oh, 5'7" maybe? With blue or green eyes? RU Ready: yep and blue Naked2: Damn. Well, meet the midget. 5'2-1/2", 112 lbs., but nicely muscled—I hit the weight room frequently…RU Ready: sorry to disappoint you…! Naked2: No, I'm not disappointed! I love 5'7", blue eyes, blond hair. Sorry if I came off that way. I hope you aren't disappointed… RU Ready: You sound good. You probably feel good Naked2:

Why don't you touch me and see? RU Ready: My time is almost up. I have 10 minutes left on my account Naked2: We could make it a quickie RU Ready: Okay, let's go. What do you want? Naked2: I like touching, kissing, sucking, licking...RU Ready: So do I. Let's do it together. I kiss your face, gently all over Naked2: I'm licking your neck, just behind your ears, trailing my tongue softly RU Ready: All over, then down your neck, my hands move up to the sash on your robe Naked2: Softly my tongue leaves your ears, my hands move to your waist, your naked skin soft beneath my fingers RU Ready: I undo the sash and rip the cloth from your body. My hands slide into your shorts and feel your wetness trickle Naked2: Ahhh, this feels sooo goood. How much time is left? RU Ready: About 7 minutes Naked2: Hurry! You're in my shorts, and I'm playing with your nipples. They are so tight and erect, it makes me... RU Ready: Ready for you. Get those pants off, now! Naked2: Okay, they're off. RU Ready: Now lie down and I'm going to go down on you. Spread your legs, ahh that's it. Here I come... Naked2: Ooooh Baby...that's it. Your tongue moving like lightning, so fast and strong RU Ready: And you are dripping, man, yes you are. Oh, I'm tasting you. You are goood. Do you like being sucked and then fucked? Or maybe fucked and sucked? Naked2: Whatever you want, I'm in agony. Just do it before we go off line... RU Ready: Okay, then I'm gonna strap on my fave and we are gonna fly, baby...fuck you inside and lick your tits. Then I'm gonna suck your cunt until you... Oh, the little light's blinking...I've got 3 minutes left. Here I come... Naked2: No, here I come, and it's major. Man, I am so wet. You going inside, in and out. I've got my legs strangling you... RU Ready: You are hot. I can't keep up with you. I'm pumping as fast as I can and you look like you're going to explode. I've got to go down now and taste your cream before it all goes... Naked2: Taste it, baby. RU Ready: Shove your cunt right in my face. That's it, oh boy, you are almost there Naked2: Almost there, god, I am RU Ready: Coming Naked2: Coming, coming...ahhhh. I have just screamed the loudest scream ever... RU Ready: Coming some more... Naked2: No, I can't, I'm finished, I'm exhausted RU Ready: Good thing. One minute left to say good-bye and stuff Naked2: God, that was incredible. I actually did come just sitting here at the keyboard RU Ready: So did I Naked2: When are you going on-line again? RU Ready: When my account's clear. Around the 22nd Naked2: Till then... RU Ready: I'll be in touch. Bye Naked2: Bye Instant Message From 38DTits 38DTits: Hey, Naked2. Do you like big tits...I bet I could make you come Naked2: Try me

Open House

It was 9:30 P.M. Monday evening as Yvonne pulled into the drive. God, what a long day. And it wasn't over yet. Being a ten-million dollar sales agent for the largest real estate company in the Philadelphia area was nice—the income was six figures, she had a Mercedes, and every year the company treated her to a trip in the Bahamas—but the days were thirty hours long! Yvonne sighed as she thought about the work that remained for today. She needed to call her relo buyers from Connecticut to let them know their contract was approved on the $525,000 custom house in Chester Springs; she had to call her seller on Monk Road in Gladwyne and try to talk him into a price reduction; and she had to return a call from an agent from another company who was bringing in an offer on the Society Hill townhouse and had some questions. And she hadn't even checked her voice mail yet! God, what a long day....

By the time Yvonne finished calling everyone who couldn't wait, it was 12:45 A.M. Time for bed. She checked her Day-Timer to see what was on the agenda for tomorrow. Maybe if I can sleep till eight I'll feel like working out in the morning, she mused. Hot damn! There was nothing in the book for tomorrow but a pre-inspection at 6 P.M. with some buyers who were settling Wednesday at 10. Guess she'd be missing the Wednesday sales meeting. So...Tuesday morning work-out? Sounding pretty good... "Shit—I forgot it's Brokers Open day," she cursed. It was tradition. Every Tuesday all the brokers held open houses for agents and brokers on their new listings and those "dead" listings they were trying to breathe some life into. And there was a new listing that an agent named Gail Allen from Brand-X had over in Chadds Ford near the Brandywine Battlefield that Yvonne just had to see. She had these transferees from New York—Stirling Drug buyers—and they were dying for something with ground, maybe old-country style. Chadds Ford was just the place. Home of the Wyeths (N.C., Andrew, Jamie). An expensive artists colony. In Chadds Ford, you could get something old, maybe restored, and with ample ground—four to six acres, maybe more—for between

$500,000 and $1,000,000. Well, the open wouldn't start until 11:00—she'd have plenty of time to get a good work-out in, make some more calls and then go.

Morning—sun creeping through the mini-blinds, making a bizarre pattern on the floor and wall. Yvonne rolled over, careful not to squish the kitten, and got up. It's great having a cat in the bed—they purr, nuzzle up next to you, and are always happy with you, especially when you feed them, she thought. Better than a lover. Who and when was the last guy in her bed? Jon? Yes, and that was seven months ago. Right after Christmas when business was a little slow. Well, she might have had a good year business-wise, but it was a bad year for fucking. Make a note in the Day-Timer: get some fucking in before Labor Day. She smiled at the thought of her secretary finding her note in her Day-Timer. Then she thought about that last night with Jon. He was an account executive with a medical supply company, and between his traveling and her business, they both had been extremely beat. Especially after the holiday stress. She had been too tired and he had snapped at her. "You're always too tired. You've made enough money selling real estate. Why don't you take a sabbatical? We could spend more time together. You could cook. You love to cook, you know. Maybe I could see what it's like to have a wife."

Yvonne glared at him and said, "If it's a wife you want, you're sleeping in the wrong bed. I enjoy what I'm doing. Why should I have to give it up just so you can have me greet you at the door with your slippers and a martini? Maybe I'm the one who needs a wife. I should put an ad in the paper." After about a week, Jon had come over to clean out the closet, and that was that.

She lingered over coffee and the paper, went to the gym, completed her workout, showered and changed. "Shouldn't have had that second cup of coffee. Now I'm late," she cursed as she dried her hair. Her hair was shoulder length, blonde and straight. Needs a perm. "When do I have time to get one," she sighed. She glanced at her watch: 11:45. She would have to make her calls from the car en route to the open house. Thank God for the car phone.

Yvonne was still talking on the phone when she pulled up the long, winding drive of the house in Chadds Ford. She was not paying attention, she was engrossed in the conversation which was becoming an argument. "Look, Gus, this is an excellent offer. These people are more than qualified and they want the house. You yourself said you want to get out as quickly as possible. With the possibility of rates going up and all that Wall Street bullshit, do you really think it's wise to just flat-out reject these people with no counter-offer? You've had no offers in five months, and you wouldn't lower the price as I recommended. Do you want to keep carrying two mortgages? Think about it." She was steamed. People could be so obtuse. She concluded the conversation with a promise from Gus to think about it and get back to her, turned the ignition off and opened the door. And then she noticed. The little walking bridge over the stream that ran in front. The ducks in the stream. The majestic house, crafted in stone with four chimneys, rising on top of the hill. Wow. This was perfect. Absolutely perfect. Perfect for her people from New York. She was just about to get on the phone and call them when she stopped herself, saying: you should see the inside. It might be a $775,000 dump. Better go in.

She opened the front door and walked into a sea of agents. It seemed like the entire Board of Realtors was here. Yvonne wondered which one was Gail—she had never met her or had a transaction with her. Well, she'd find her as soon as the tour was over. Yvonne looked around the foyer and was pleased. No "handyman's special" here. This was circa 1850, with major restoration. Wide crown moldings throughout, a fireplace with the most exquisite mantle in the living room—four fireplaces total including one in the master bedroom. And what a kitchen! Brick walls, brick fireplace with a hearth and bake oven, oh, she couldn't believe her good fortune! She would have to get on the phone right away. Just as she was turning to leave the kitchen, a voice behind her said, "You haven't had anything to eat yet. We have a fabulous gourmet spread in the family room."

Yvonne turned and she was eye level with a pair of beautiful chocolate brown eyes in a very attractive face framed by luscious dark brown hair that fell just below her ears. Yvonne found herself staring a little longer than she would care to admit, and then, as if by some remote command, she stuck out her hand and said, "Hi, I'm Yvonne Burns. I don't think we've ever met."

The dark haired stranger's hand enveloped Yvonne's as she replied, "I'm Gail Allen. I've heard so much about you. There are fact sheets and brochures on the dry sink in the dining room. I'll be glad to answer any questions you might have."

Yvonne found she couldn't take her eyes off Gail as she went into the foyer to greet some newcomers. Why haven't I run into her before? she thought. She absently walked into the dining room, picked up a brochure and fact sheet and was trying to digest the information. She couldn't concentrate—the words seemed to congeal into a long, unintelligible mass. She was a little disturbed at this unusual lapse in her abilities. Nothing ever distracted her. May as well eat something. She headed towards the family room where the luncheon was waiting.

Gail was shaking hands and making small talk with agents in the foyer. It was fairly common knowledge in the real estate community that Gail was a lesbian. As she stood in the foyer, Gail's eyes kept wandering around the room, hoping to catch a glimpse of Yvonne. She thought: She's gorgeous. I wonder what it's like to have dinner with her? To work out with her? To sleep with her? But she's also straight. So that rules out sleeping with her. But the rest...hmmm. Uh oh. Reality check. Yvonne probably knew all about Gail's sexual proclivities, and what made Gail think she'd even agree to something so innocuous as dinner? With the volume of business she does, and the amount of time she devotes every day to her business, having dinner with the town dyke probably wouldn't rate high on her list of things to do. Still, Gail was enjoying the view from the foyer as Yvonne walked in from the family room. Couldn't hurt to look, anyway.

Yvonne walked over to a sofa in the living room and sat down, plate in hand. As she toyed with her pasta salad, her mind worked feverishly trying to recall all that she knew about Gail Allen. She really didn't know the woman at all—she'd heard through the grapevine bits and pieces and wondered how much of it was true. She was gay, someone said. She'd lived with a woman for five years, and the woman had moved away out of state last year. Yvonne remembered a Board of Realtors luncheon she had attended not that long ago, and Gail's name had come up in the conversation. Her office mate Marty had remarked, "She just needs a good man. That'll cure her. One night with me and she'll never look at a pussy again—except her own."

Yvonne had smiled as the others in the group laughed heartily, but how had she felt then? She hadn't really liked Marty's remark, but she just went along with it. Like I always do—don't rock the boat, she thought to herself now as she fumbled with the pasta. What did it matter? Gail wasn't hurting anyone and she hadn't noticed Gail staring at her for any length of time. She'd been the one doing the staring, Yvonne remembered now. There was something she couldn't quite get, couldn't quite put her finger on. She had found Gail attractive, certainly. She hadn't expected to find Gail attractive. And maybe that was it—she wasn't prepared to find anything likable about Gail. Why? Just because she was a dyke? She didn't look like a dyke—she wasn't drop-dead gorgeous, but she was good-looking. At least not like what dykes were supposed to look like. Instantly Yvonne recalled the image of Mrs. Benson, her high school gym teacher. She was married, but all the girls said she was really a lesbo—she just married to keep mouths shut. And she looked the part—short, stocky, close-cropped hair. Mrs. Benson even held her cigarette like a man, between thumb and forefinger. Yvonne tried to draw some parallel between Mrs. Benson and Gail Allen, and she was having a tough time. Well, it's the 90s and all-or-nothing is the way it's supposed to be, she thought, and cleaned up her plate. Time to go. Better say good-bye to Gail, get back to the office and call the Rosenbergs in New York. They were going to love this house.

Gail was in the foyer talking with a tall, dark-haired agent Yvonne recognized as someone from Gail's office, Bernie-something-or-other. Yvonne walked up to Gail, extended her hand and said: "This is a marvelous listing. I just might have someone for this, so you'll probably be hearing from me."

Gail shook her hand and said, "Thanks for coming. I'll be looking for your call."

Yvonne started down the front steps, then turned and

impulsively said, "Why don't we have dinner tomorrow night? I'm very positive about these people, and we might be able to iron out some details before they come in this weekend. Plus, it'll give us a chance to get to know each other."

Wow. Gail fought the urge to look up at the sky and say, "Yes!" Instead she said, "Let me call you later after I've checked my schedule, but as of now dinner sounds fine."

Yvonne left, and Gail continued to stare after her as she pretended to be listening to Bernie talking about his problems with an appraiser. Whatever made Yvonne ask her to dinner? Don't get yourself all worked up about it—she just wants to talk business, she thought. Time to clean up anyway—Open House is over.

As promised, Gail called Yvonne when she returned to the office. Dinner would be no problem. They made arrangements to meet at the Towne Hall, a fashionable place in nearby West Chester, at 7:00 the next night. Yvonne waited until she got home that evening to call the Rosenbergs and tell them about Gail's listing. They seemed excited, and Yvonne told them she'd make an appointment for 10:00 Saturday morning. After Yvonne hung up the phone, she sat down on the bed, took off her shoes and then lay down, still fully dressed in her suit. What a day. She just lay there, mentally reliving every moment, especially the moment she had invited Gail to dinner. You're just curious, you've never been up close and personal with a lesbian before, she thought. Yvonne had to admit she was curious, just a little. She had seen movies—she pretty much knew what they did in bed anyway. And what they did together, well you could get that with a guy. They would go down on you. Yvonne rolled over on her stomach, propped herself up with her elbows and rested her chin on her fists. "But it must be different," she mouthed the words silently. And then she rolled over on her back and lifted up her blouse, then wriggled out of her skirt. She started touching herself, her breasts, feeling her way down her abdomen to her thighs, then her hands moved between her legs. Even as she was arousing herself, Yvonne was still thinking, "It's different, to feel a woman's touch, to touch a woman." For if she wanted to know a woman's caress or what it felt like to touch a woman, why not touch herself? Surely she knew what it was all about now. So, no problem with dinner tomorrow.

Yvonne was late, as usual, and she walked into the Towne Hall feeling a little guilty about it. She saw Gail at the bar in the lounge, walked over and said, "I'm sorry I'm late, but it's something I can't ever seem to grow out of."

Gail just smiled a little half smile and said, "The second coming of Burns and Allen and you're late?"

Seeing Yvonne's wilted look, Gail quickly said, "I was just kidding. Really. No problem. I'm used to it by now. I called and made reservations for 7:30, so actually you're early. What would you like to drink? On me."

Yvonne said, "Scotch and water," and sat down next to Gail. What had she meant by 'I'm used to it by now?'

Maybe her girlfriend-lover—whatever the term was—had always been late.

Her drink arrived and Yvonne took a deep sip. Steeling herself for the big night out with the dyke. No, what did she have to be worried about? Yvonne looked at Gail and said, "It's good to finally meet you after all this time knowing about you." Gail looked quizzically at her, and Yvonne instantly backtracked, saying, "Well, I meant, after all this time I've heard of you but never met you." No, that didn't sound right either. Yvonne sighed and said, "I know what I'm trying to say but I'm not saying it very well. I've heard a lot about you and it's nice to finally meet you." Whew.

Gail laughed and said, "Geez, I thought you were going soft on me and trying to tell me that you know I'm gay and it's okay."

Yvonne had started to raise her glass to her lips, but she stopped midway, dumbfounded. "Well, that's not was I was trying to say, but now that you mention it, it is okay with me."

Gail looked at her and said, "Thank you. And it's okay with me that you're straight."

Yvonne had to laugh at that point. Just then the waiter came over and motioned them to their table. They picked up their drinks and followed.

Seated at the table, Yvonne started to pull her cigarettes out of her purse, then remembered to ask, "Mind if I smoke? I hope this is the smoking area."

Gail replied, "I was hoping you were a smoker. So am

I. Of course I booked the smoking area. Can I give you a light?"

Yvonne retrieved the pack, pulled a cigarette out, placed it in her fingers and leaned slightly forward. Gail had picked up matches from the ashtray, struck one and leaned forward toward Yvonne. As Yvonne held out her hand with the cigarette in it, Gail gently grasped her hand and brought it toward her, cigarette just touching the match. A whiff of freshly burning cigarette permeated the air. Yvonne brought her lips to the cigarette still clasped in her hand and drew deeply. Gail's fingers lingered on Yvonne's hand, feeling its softness. Then she let go. "Sorry about that. I sometimes like to see if straight people feel as good as we do."

Yvonne smiled and said, "Did I pass the test?"

Gail looked at her, taking a very long drag on her cigarette and said, "Definitely yes."

They had a marathon dinner—Yvonne couldn't remember ever a dinner in which she was so captured by the conversation. They went through one bottle of wine, and then they had Bailey's over ice for dessert. Somehow during the dinner, they managed to review the details of the house in Chadds Ford. Yvonne had written notes down as Gail briefed her. Good thing she brought her notebook—she would never have remembered after the Bailey's.

As they sipped their Bailey's, Yvonne said to Gail, "So who are you with now?"

Gail's fingers were playing with the stem of her glass

and she said, "No one right now. I was in a relationship for five years but that's over." She looked down at the table and Yvonne thought for a minute that she was going to cry.

"She hurt you, didn't she," said Yvonne, wanting to reach out and touch her hand but not daring.

Gail said: "We hurt each other at times. But in the end she left without ever telling me why. That's what hurt the most."

Gail's eyes met hers and Yvonne saw pain, but something else she couldn't figure out. "Hey, why don't we get out of here and go somewhere where we can talk? That is, if you want to. I live close by. Why don't you follow me and we can have coffee at my place," Yvonne said, mentally wondering if she had any coffee. There was always Wawa.

They pulled into Yvonne's driveway, Yvonne in her Mercedes and Gail in her Maxima. Fearing the worst, Yvonne had stopped at Wawa and brought home two 20 oz. Chocolate Macadamia Nut coffees. After inspecting the kitchen cabinets, Yvonne was thankful she had decided to stop. She was out of coffee.

So there they were, sitting in the living room, drinking their gourmet coffees. Now what? Yvonne spoke first: "I just want you to know, you're the first, well, gay person I've known personally. I mean, I've known of other people, but I never had the opportunity to be close to them, to get to know them, and you are the first."

Gail smiled that little half smile and said, "Well, do I pass the test?"

Yvonne's blood was pounding through her veins. What's happening to me? I want to touch her, to hold her, and I don't know why. Yvonne heard herself saying, "Yes, you do." Yvonne reached out her hand to Gail's face, feeling her softness, the sharp lines of her jaw. And then she felt Gail's hand on hers, fingers tracing the tips of her own fingers, running down her palm.

Gail said: "Please tell me if I'm wrong, but I get this vibe that you're just the slightest bit curious about me. Believe me, nothing will happen. Unless you want it to."

Yvonne's fingers clasped around Gail's. She was unable to answer, could only nod her head. What was she doing? Somehow she didn't feel panic about the situation—in fact, everything felt good. Maybe I should just relax and enjoy the moment, she thought. But then the panic struck: what if we actually do it? What am I supposed to do?

Gail pulled her around and said, "Am I making you uncomfortable? I'll leave if you want. Talk to me."

Yvonne looked at her, drew a deep breath and said, "I'm not sure, but I've felt this feeling ever since I met you, that I wondered what it would be like to sleep with you. I don't know why I'm feeling this way—it may be curiosity—and it's definitely not like me, but there it is. My problem is that I've never ever been with a woman before and I wouldn't know what to do." Yvonne looked at the floor.

Gail's hand was on her face, under her chin, pulling her up to meet her gaze. "I'll help you. It won't be that hard. It's like we take turns. I make love to you, then you reciprocate. Except you won't have to, not this first time, unless you want to. I wouldn't ask that of you. And if you feel like you have to stop at anytime, I will. Just tell me. But it's not over until you're satisfied."

Yvonne looked at her. How different than being with a man.

Gail's hand moved up her face, caressing her, then around her face entirely, feeling every part of her face—lips, nose, eyelids, ears. Instinctively Yvonne brought her hand up to touch Gail. So soft, so delicate, this woman's skin. No five o'clock stubble. Yvonne closed her eyes and moaned softly as Gail's hand moved down her neck, lightly touching, stroking her. Then she felt a hand on her breast and Yvonne felt a bolt of electricity move through her body. Gail's hand slowly played with her, teasing her nipple, tugging gently, then pinching just a little. As Yvonne moaned a little more, Gail brought her other hand up to caress the other breast. Quickly Gail began unbuttoning Yvonne's blouse, removed it, and then unfastening her brassiere, loosening her breasts. Her lips moved across Yvonne's chest, coming to rest on her breasts where they endlessly sucked and teased her. Tongue flicking lightly, then harder across her nipples. Yvonne lay back on the couch. This felt so good. She was dimly aware of her own hands grasping Gail's head and guiding it down away from her breasts, across her abdomen. She felt Gail reach behind her and undo the clasp of her skirt, then pull at her zipper and finally removing her skirt, then her slip, and then her shoes and pantyhose, all the while continuing to kiss and torment her breasts. Then Gail slid her hands into Yvonne's underpants, feeling the silkiness, the wetness within, and slid her pants down over her ankles. Yvonne reached her hand into Gail's blouse, unbuttoning and trying to get the material off. Gail said, "Not now. Later." Then she brought her hand up and trailed a wet finger across her belly and Yvonne was amazed at her own wetness. Gail lay on top of Yvonne, parted her legs and began her downward journey, kissing every inch of Yvonne along the way. She ran her fingers along her thighs, and lightly kissed along the path her fingers left. She then began kissing up her thighs, her lips finally landing on Yvonne's clit. Gail raised her head and said:

"All you all right? If you want me to stop, just tell me. It's okay."

Yvonne looked at her through half-lidded eyes and said: "Are you crazy?" And she pushed Gail's head back down between her legs.

Gail's tongue moved slowly back and forth across her, sending jolts of lightening through Yvonne. As Yvonne began moaning softly and moving into her, Gail began moving faster, her hands gripping Yvonne's thighs. Yvonne's mind was a whirlwind—had she ever felt like this before and how and when and how long did it last?—thoughts were running haywire. She felt herself begin to tense—Gail must have noticed too, because she gripped Yvonne's hands and said, "Relax, just enjoy it. I want to make you feel good."

Gail moved up and kissed Yvonne, her tongue moving lightly across her lips, then inside gently, exploring. Long deep kisses. Yvonne was becoming more aroused even though Gail had stopped touching her. Yvonne grasped Gail's face with both hands and said, "Now. Or I'm afraid I won't make it."

Gail went back down on her quickly, her tongue dancing across Yvonne's clit and soon Yvonne was riding to the top of the Ferris wheel. She felt the first wave come over her, and she thought she was done. But Gail was still going, gently, and Yvonne could feel an incredible second wave engulfing her. She wanted more and pushed herself further into Gail. Her back was arched, her breasts standing erect and Gail's fingers were playing, twisting, kneading. Yvonne was riding a wave that would rival a tsunami, and she crashed violently, collapsing into the couch, Gail collapsing with her, on top of her. Yvonne felt as though she couldn't move and didn't want to. They lay there together, exhausted.

Finally, Gail rolled off of Yvonne, sat up and said, "You okay?"

Yvonne dreamily looked at her and said, "I never thought cooperating with Brand-X would be so good."

Gail smiled and said, "Mind if we continue this transaction in the bedroom? The sofa's a little cramped."

Yvonne sat up and said, "You read my mind." She ran her fingers down Gail's arm, Gail pulled her in and held her close. They stood up, Yvonne leading Gail into the hall. They entered the bedroom and sat down on the bed, Yvonne starting to undo the buttons on Gail's blouse.

Gail caught her hand and said, "Are you sure?"

Yvonne said, "Come on, real estate lady. I liked the offer you presented me. Now I have a counter offer for you." Gail leaned back and smiled as Yvonne continued undressing her. Real Estate. What a business…

Raining You

It's raining outside. Big drops, splattering against my window pane. Like the tears that made their way down My face when you said we were through. Sometimes it seems like we've been Saying good-bye since we met. But it's raining outside. Raining you. The first day we met It was raining. Big drops, drenching us in their passion. And we were full of passion. Unexplored, soon to be fulfilled. I held you close as we ran through the water Searching for a dry space. It was raining, raining you. In my car, I felt something about you That I hadn't realized I was able to feel. And you knew, long before I did How I would feel about you. I could feel your skin through Your clothes, so wet we were. And now it's raining, Raining you. I do not see myself As lovable, though I believe You do. I'm too technical, too rooted in books and facts. But I see you, so romantic And I feel romantic. It must be raining. Raining you. Late at night, I often Dream of you. In my dreams, we are lying together In the middle of the night. On cool satin sheets Though our bodies are very hot. I am soaked with your wetness It is raining you.

Margaritas and Bikinis

"Take the L out of Lover and it's over…" Martha Davis from the Motels was wailing from the ghetto blaster, with some hefty competition from BJ. It was summer 1984, Rehoboth Beach, Delaware. The sun was searing through the clouds on the beach with the precision of a laser. I was with my "group," the usual crowd I hung out with every year at Rehoboth. We picked our spot on the gay beach, a.k.a. "Poodle Beach," every weekend and planted our "Grab a Heiney" flag as though we had just climbed Mt. Everest or landed on the moon and were merely staking our claim to that precise spot on the beach. No trespassing allowed, unless one met the criteria, which could be anything we imagined. One definitely had to be musically astute—we would not tolerate the blasé offerings of regular radio. This had to be special—being dykes, we were not especially interested in the sissyfag selections of "Judy Garland Live at Carnegie Hall" or "Liza with a Z." Something along the lines of Laura Branigan "Self Control," the Pretenders "Akron" or "Thumbelina" would be our ticket.

There I was, plastered in my chair, listening but not really listening, because I was too busy watching. I watched everything that moved, and people are especially fun to watch. And then I saw her. She was walking by the water, just letting the icy water tease her toes. I found that I couldn't breathe—she was striking. Blonde hair—it's a killer every time with me. But it wasn't long—she had it short and spiky. And the rest of her, well I was too far away to really see. Have to get a closer view. Thank God it was too early for cocktails—by 11:00 someone in our group, usually BJ, would say, "Is it 12:00 yet?" And Big Pearl (she was well endowed) would reply, "Nope." And then I would decide for everyone by saying "Well, it's 12:00 somewhere in the world," and the sound of cans being opened would reverberate like a twenty-one-gun salute. But it was only 10:00. I was sober now and it was a good thing because I had just decided to get up and go for a walk. Or a jog, since this beautiful thing was moving very quickly down the beach. If I didn't hurry she'd be gone from sight.

"Excuse me, and where do you think you're going?" cackled BJ.

"For a walk—it's too hot," I said. And off I started, ignoring BJ's pleas to come back, they couldn't start cocktails without me. "Go ahead and start if you want—you all know how to open a can, for Chrissakes," I hollered as I started into a slow jog. I was so thankful I had given up smoking and taken up jogging. If I was still puffing those cancer sticks there's no way I'd have lasted this long into my jog. Damn, where did she go? I had been so busy fending off BJ that I had lost sight of her in the sea of bodies on the beach. I stopped and scanned the beach, the chairs, the towels, the people in the water—she was gone. Shit. "Goddamn you, BJ," I cursed out loud. I hadn't been with anyone for almost a year now, and the one person, the one singular person I found attractive enough to get me off my ass, well, she had disappeared. Thanks to BJ. No, I take that back. Things happen for a reason, and I'm not into blaming anyone for my life, or lack of it at this point.

Dejectedly, I decided to continue my journey, hoping against hope that I'd see her. Well, if not her, maybe someone else will turn up. And if nobody turns up, then I'll just have to be content with eyeing all the bodies baking like salmon on towels. As I strolled down by the water to get into the cool sand, past little groupings on the beach I heard a strange mix of music—Maria Callas, Donna Summer, Barbra Streisand, Liza Minelli. Somehow the diverse sounds and styles managed to blend without too much dissonance. As I walked farther and farther the crowds dissipated and I realized I was going the wrong way—the end of the beach was in sight and I could see houses ahead. There's no way I would find her now.

For some reason I kept walking toward the houses. There was a little path through the brush and I came out to a cul-de-sac. There were three houses ahead, and if I turned right, the street would take me back towards gay beach. I didn't have any shoes on, and when I planted my foot on the macadam I let out a yelp. It was sizzling. I would not be able to walk up the street. Time to turn around and go back the way I came. As I turned around, my eyes focused for a split second on the first house and I thought I saw something moving on the porch. I stopped and squinted—it was her! I couldn't believe my good fortune. She was walking down the front stairs, walking toward me.

"I heard you cry out and I didn't know if you needed some help," she said.

I couldn't look at her, so I turned my gaze toward the beach and said, "I got lost walking on the beach, and I'm afraid I didn't bring my walking shoes with me and the macadam burnt my foot. I'll just have to go back the way I came." I was starting to get a cramp in my neck from looking the other way, so I turned my head around and faced her. Up close, she was even more stunning. She kind of had an Annie Lennox type hair cut, and her face was sort of Nordic looking—high cheekbones, blue eyes. She had a bikini top on and a towel wrapped around her waist and a pair of black hi-top Converse Chuck Taylor All-Stars on her feet. No socks.

"Why don't you come in and I'll lend you a pair of sandals? The sand might be hotter now and you could still burn your feet."

I nodded my head, dumbstruck. After walking what I had determined to be the wrong way on the beach, I had found her after all. Yes, things do happen for a reason. I wasn't so mad at BJ anymore.

Because I couldn't walk in the street, we walked back toward the beach. "Come around the back way. It's grassy and you'll be all right." We poked our way through tall grass and came to the rear of the house. It was a beautiful three story beach house, with a wrap-around deck on each floor. We went up the steps to the first level, she opened the wooden screen door and said, "Come in." I followed her into as gorgeous a living room as I had ever seen in Architectural Digest. High cathedral ceiling, massive floor to ceiling stone fireplace, red clay tile floor—it was marvelous. I was so taken with the interior that I didn't hear her move next to me. Her hand was on my shoulder and I felt an old, familiar tingling through my body. I turned around and she said, "Would you like something to drink? How about a margarita?"

I glanced at my watch. It was 11:30. Wow, I had been gone a long time. I looked at her and said, "I usually don't drink before 12:00. But, hey, it's 12:00 somewhere in the world, right?"

She laughed and said, "I've heard that line so many times, I thought I would die if I heard it again. But coming from you it sounds funnier than I ever thought it would be. I have a pitcher in the refrigerator. I'll be right back."

She turned around and went towards the kitchen. I followed her saying, "This is a marvelous house. Are you renting for the summer?"

"No, this house is mine. It's my family's summer home."

Family home. Well, that's that. Husband. Two, three kids, in-laws. End of my fantasy. Well, I'll have that margarita, get some shoes and go. But what was she doing on the gay beach? There was an island in the kitchen with a Jenn-Air and some bar stools. I sat down and figured I may as well find out all the details. "So is your family out for the day? The place seems deserted except for you."

"I have no family anymore. My parents built this house, and they're both dead. They both died within a year of each other, both from cancer, and they deeded it to me before they died so we could avoid paying as much inheritance tax as possible." She handed me my drink and I took a big sip as I comprehended the information. The drink was delicious. And she had put salt on the glass. Without even asking me if I liked salt on my glass, which I do.

"I'm sorry to hear about your parents. My father died when I was seventeen, right before I graduated from high school. It was very sudden—heart attack, and we were all just stunned. It must have been hard for you having to watch them die in front of your eyes."

She looked at me and said, "You're very perceptive. It was extremely hard. Many times I wished they would just die instantly, like a heart attack, just to get it over with. I wasn't sure I could stand to watch them. But it's over now and they're at peace." She picked up her glass and said, "Come on in the living room. Let's sit and talk." I followed her to the sofa and she sat down, pointing to the cushion next to her.

Seated comfortably, I took another sip and told her how good the margarita was, adding, "You even gave me salt without asking. How did you know I liked salt?"

She set her glass down and leaned into me and said, "I could tell."

Just like that. Then she ran her fingers down one side of my face, down my neck, then up the other side. I was getting that tingle again, only worse. I'm going to come right here and now and all she did was touch my face, I thought. Boy, it had been a long time. I was thinking about asking her why she was at the beach but something told me to let it go. I had a feeling she'd been to this beach before.

She started to kiss me on the lips, gently, then moving down my neck, behind my ear. I closed my eyes and let out a small sigh. This felt so good. I put my hands on her waist and I felt the towel slip. I let my hands rest on her waist, then they moved down to her hips. She was naked, and had been when she came out to see me in the street! Aroused even further by this revelation, I sighed louder and my hands moved between her thighs to feel her wetness. By now her lips were on my chest and she reached around to undo the clasp on my top, freeing my breasts. She moved behind me and I could hear her undo her top. The next thing I felt were her breasts on my back as her cunt rubbed my ass. I started to turn around but she said, "Stay there." The tone of her voice sounded rather authoritative, so I obeyed. I always do as I am told.

Her hands were stroking my breasts, pulling, playing with my nipples, while she rubbed against me from behind. I was dying, hoping she'd turn me over and go down on me. I could feel my wetness start to trickle down my legs. One hand went between my legs, her fingers inside of me and she teased me a bit, making me flow even more. My sighs had turned to loud moaning. She said, "Turn over," and I just rolled, arching as I did. Her tongue was on my breasts, licking, sucking, and her hand stayed inside me. Then her fingers moved outside to my clit which was by now completely soaked and begging for her. She continued to suck my nipples while torturing my clit and her other hand slid inside of me and she began fucking me. I hadn't felt anything quite like this and I tried to hold on and lose myself in the incredible sensations pulsing through my body. But I was a little out of practice and I came almost instantly. Her mouth moved up to mine, kissing me gently.

"It's been a while, hasn't it?" she whispered.

"Yes, almost a year. I'm sorry that I couldn't keep up with you, but it was absolutely wonderful. Maybe we could try again."

She moved her head away from me and she got up, smiling. "Think you can find the bedroom? I'll bring a fresh pitcher...and the salt."

The Intruder

The freeway was packed full with cars barely crawling along at twenty-five miles per hour. I had just about had it with sitting in traffic; my nerves were shot, I was irritable and I was having trouble with my cellular phone. Maybe the battery was dying—I cursed myself for buying one of those portable hand-held jobs. Either way, I couldn't get through to let my lover know I was going to be late getting home. Before I left that morning she had asked me what time I would be home. I was thirty minutes late. I was pissed.

Finally I reached my exit, and after hitting nearly

every red light on the main road, I pulled into my driveway. I noticed that my lover's car wasn't there; maybe she was stuck in traffic too. I thought about calling my voice mail to see if she had left a message, but then remembering my phone troubles I said to myself the hell with it, I'll call when I get inside, and I walked to the front door. The outside light wasn't on and I was having trouble finding the deadbolt keyhole. We needed to get a motion sensor on that front door light. Maybe when the temperature was a little warmer, I'd get out my Time-Life repair book and figure out how to do it. I was looking forward to a nice hot bath and a glass of wine, even if I'd be by myself.

I turned the key in the deadbolt, withdrew it and inserted it into the door handle. After unlocking the handle, I turned the knob and started to remove the key from the handle. As I stepped inside, my right hand went instinctively up to flick the outside light switch on so when my lover got home she would at least be able to see. I then moved my hand to the next switch to turn on the living room light and all of a sudden a hand clamped over my mouth. "Don't scream," the voice behind me said. Something was being slipped over my head—a cloth or bandanna. All I knew was that it covered my eyes and I was plunged into total darkness.

"Put your hands behind your back," the disembodied voice said, and I obeyed. Now my hands were bound with a piece of cloth. "Upstairs," the voice said.

"I can't see," I managed to croak, my heart racing.

"I'll guide you from behind," said the voice. I felt hands on my waist and I was turned around and pointed in a different direction. "Move," the voice said. I began to walk, unsure of myself. I moved slowly, afraid I would trip or run into something. The coffee table? Where was it? I tried to picture the room layout.

"You're at the stairs." The hands moved from my waist to my lower back. "I've got you. You won't fall." I gingerly placed my foot on the first step, then the next. It seemed like an hour, but I finally made it to the top step. "This way," the voice said. I felt myself being turned in a different direction. Where were we going? The bedroom?

"Stop. Okay, now let me turn you this way. Slowly sit down."

I did as directed and realized that I was sitting on the edge of my bed.

"I'm going to untie your hands."

I felt relief as the bonds were loosened.

"Now lie down on your back."

Again I did as I was told. I felt the hands grasp both wrists and pull my arms over my head. My wrists were bound again and I realized that I was being tied to the bedposts.

"Would you like something to drink?" the voice asked me.

Wow. Such concern about my well-being. I said, "Yes." My throat was parched. I felt a hand under my head raising my head and something smooth and curved touched my lips.

"It's water. Drink."

I drank tentatively at first, then I took in several mouthfuls. I felt the glass leave my lips. Hands touched my face, tracing my lips. I felt something touch my lips—other lips. Soft, smooth. I did not return the kisses, but tried to move my face away. "It will be easier if you don't fight," the voice said. "Otherwise I may have to hurt you." I felt hands gliding down my body, touching my breasts through my clothes. I realized that I still had my suit jacket on. No wonder I was roasting. The hands began unbuttoning my blouse. My breasts are small and I hardly ever wear a bra unless absolutely necessary. I felt fingers grasp my right nipple. The fingers tugged very lightly. My nipple instantly became hard. All of a sudden both nipples were being tweaked. At first I tried to move away, but then I felt a weight on my stomach and I knew the intruder was sitting on top of me. "Just relax and enjoy it," the voice said. I had no choice now. I couldn't move at all. The fingers continued to work and I became aware of an ache between my legs and a tingling sensation. The weight moved off of me, and my skirt was lifted. My stockings were being rolled down, off came my shoes, stockings next. A hand tugged my underwear down and over my feet. Hands were on my legs, moving up my thighs. Again that ache between my legs, and I felt something roll down my thigh. I was becoming wet! The hands moved up and I felt fingers touch my clit. The tingling intensified and my leg involuntarily jerked upwards. I knew I had hit something with my knee and I heard a small moan above me.

Fingers were playing with my clit now, rubbing very slowly, and there were fingers playing with both breasts. I lay very still, trying not to move. I was going crazy—so many wonderful sensations coursing through my body. Something else had joined the fingers down there—a tongue, lashing, swirling, probing. The bedsheets underneath me were becoming soaked with my own wetness. The tongue and fingers moved faster, faster, the fingers worked my nipple faster and faster. My body began rocking in odd, yet rhythmic spasms.

Oh, boy, here we go, on that magic roller coaster ride… I was in a frenzy, I knew we were coming up on that big hill, the one that would set me screaming when we made that ninety degree vertical drop. Here it is, oh man, everything's going crazy, I think I'm gonna die—no, I'm still here but I'm gonna explode instead, yes, heeeeere it comesssss….

I was spent, limp. I lay in total darkness, in wetness, small moans were coming out of my lips. I felt the hands behind my head and the bandanna was lifted. I could see!

"You were late as usual."

"I was stuck in traffic. Where's the car this time?"

"Down the street. You'd better watch your knees."

I rolled over and looked at my lover of twenty years. I gently touched the red mark my knee had left on her chin and said, "And you'd better start leaving the outside light on."

The Sauna

The club was not very crowded; it was after 8:00 P.M. Nikki had about five minutes left on the PTS Turbo 1000 Reclining Cycle, and then she would move on to the free weights. She was staring at the TV in the front; CNN Headline News was on—something about the ice-skating scandal. She was interrupted by a voice coming from her left:

"Excuse me. How do you set the program for this?" Nikki turned her attention from the TV and saw a woman seated on the PTS next to her. "I'm sorry. I've never used one of these before. Could you help me get started?"

Nikki said, "Sure," and she began explaining the bike's operation. When she was finished, the woman thanked her and began pedaling.

Well, I may as well go onto weights, Nikki thought, and she dismounted her bike, wiped the seat with her hand towel and went into the weight room.

Nikki worked a pair of twenty lb. dumbbells, doing two sets of twelve reps each of bicep curls, then overhead for two sets for the trapezoids, and so on until she had given her arms a thorough workout. She moved onto the Nautilus for pecs and chest press, lats and obliques and tricep extensions. After a brief respite to gulp some water, Nikki concentrated on her legs for the next fifteen minutes, then back to the weight room for some work on her thighs and buttocks. After she had finished the last squat and was positive her legs would give way, it was time for abs. One hundred regular sit ups, then fifty to each side. Droplets of sweat rolled freely into Nikki's eyes, blurring her vision. It's Miller time, she thought, and rolled over onto her stomach, rose and walked toward the locker room, toweling her forehead. She felt energized and at the same time drained. Her muscles had what she called a good hurt—they ached from being pushed to the brink—but when she flexed her bicep and placed her thumb and forefinger astride the mass and caressed herself, she felt pleasure in the shape. As she entered the locker room and passed the full length mirror in the entrance way, she paused for a few seconds. She loved watching herself, her body, examining every detail as though she were a sculptor planning her next piece. Gazing down the glass at herself, she saw a woman who was long, lean, angular—not at all unlike an Aubrey Beardsley or Erté etching. Standing at the mirror, scrutinizing herself, Nikki saw that her nipples were erect. She suddenly became very aware of a dull ache in her groin—must be those endorphins, she mused, and she walked to her locker and took out her workout bag. After stripping off her sweaty clothes, she grabbed her shower essentials and went into the shower area.

Club rule—must shower before using the hot tub. The hot tub would feel good today. Nikki had really worked herself hard and the pulsating jets of water were a welcome relief to her body. But one can only sit in the whirlpool so long. Nikki got out, started for the shower, then changed direction and opened the door to the sauna. Just a little heat for five minutes, she thought. She entered the room, closed the door, stepped up one level, spread out her towel and lay down on the upper bench. The thermometer read one hundred fifty degrees—not too hot, not lukewarm—just right. Soon droplets of sweat would form all over her body, running rivulets down her arms, thighs, breasts.

As Nikki relaxed, enjoying the wet heat, she again became aware of the dull ache between her legs. Lifting up her head, she noticed that her nipples were still hard, erect. After a quick glance at the small window in the door, she moved her right hand up to her right breast and ran her fingertip over the erect nipple. Electric. No, it wasn't the endorphins—she really was aroused. She tugged gently at the nipple, rolling it between thumb and forefinger, and felt the ache increase between her legs. She moved her free hand down between her legs and felt silky, smooth wetness. She started to stroke herself but stopped abruptly, remembering where she was. As she withdrew her hand, she was startled by the scraping sound of the door opening.

"Mind if I join you?"

Nikki looked up, wondering if the smell of her cunt was too strong, and saw the woman she had helped earlier with the bike. "No, come on in, the heat's fine," Nikki replied. Good, she silently thought. Maybe having a complete stranger to talk to will have the same effect as a cold shower. Nikki watched the woman as she sat on the bench. Her towel, which had been wrapped neatly around her torso, was beginning to come undone and Nikki could see her legs, no, up a little—there it was! Nikki's eyes feasted on the golden mound of hair that rested between the woman's legs. Nikki had known a few women, but she had never slept with anyone who had a blonde pussy—and here it was, staring her in the face. Her first one. Wow.

Nikki raised her eyes up and met the woman's gaze. Suddenly, she realized she had been caught staring. Now how do I explain this? thought Nikki. She coughed a small dry cough as if to clear her throat and said, "I'm sorry if I was staring. I wasn't looking at you—I was thinking about this big project I've got going at work.

My boss is killing me with so much overtime—I can't get away from it, even here at the club."

The woman laughed and said, "Yes, I know what you mean. I can't ever seem to leave my job at the office, either."

Whew. Nikki sent a small prayer of thanks. Her story had been believed.

The woman spoke again: "But it's not about work, is it? That wasn't a blank stare on your face—your eyes were directed at me. You were staring between my legs."

Nikki felt as if she would throw up. Ohmigod, what do I do now? Quick, damage control needed. Make something up.

Before she had a chance to blurt out the next lie, the woman said, "You ever see a blonde one before?"

Nikki was too embarrassed to look the woman in the eye, so she shook her head and meekly replied, "No."

"Funny, my husband had the same reaction," the woman said.

"Oh, you're married?" Nikki said with what she hoped was a smile.

"Not anymore," said the woman. "He liked other women. Which I know you do too. Otherwise, you wouldn't have looked at me the way you did."

Nikki couldn't believe what she was hearing. Still too stunned to look up, all she could manage was: "I was that obvious?"

The woman replied gently, "Yes, you were. Look at me. Now."

Nikki raised up her head, looked at the woman and saw that she was smiling.

"It's okay," the woman said.

Nikki thought: The only way I'll get through this is just to look her in the eye and tell her I'm sorry and it'll never happen again. Maybe I'll even join another club. Or at least I'll tell her that.

As Nikki was just about to speak, suddenly the woman's hand was on her shoulder. Fingers slowly caressed her shoulder, moving their way down her arm. Nikki closed her eyes. This can't be real. The heat's getting to me. How long have I been in here? As her brain struggled to process, the fingers traveled across her arm and reached her breast, finding her nipple. Nikki closed her eyes and felt the incredible sensation of fingers gently but firmly grasping, kneading, playing, pulling her. This is not happening. No way, thought Nikki. But then the woman's face drew close, and lips touched hers. Soft lips. Then a tongue, probing, tasting, seeking, invading her mouth. Hands found their way all over her body.

I'll never make it, Nikki thought. I can't stop her, and I want her. So she gave in. She brought her hands up and caught the woman's hands in her own. Fingers interlocked. Then her fingers ran up arms, down breasts, feeling and taking whatever was in their path. Nikki placed her hand on the woman's towel, pulling it aside, and she looked down and saw everything. Everything she had hoped for. Nikki managed to say, "You're wonderful," but just as she finished the woman's head was between her legs. Fingers were inside of her, stroking, pumping and the woman's tongue was grinding against her clit. Nikki didn't know what to do—she didn't have a conscious thought except how good everything felt and how many minutes it was until show time. She was wet, sopping, and she could feel the juice trickling down her legs. She reached out her hand and guided the woman's head—wow, it was just right! The tongue was at the right spot, and Nikki could feel herself climbing up, up the climax mountain and at the right moment she would hit the top and then fall off. Maybe it would be a slow death this time...maybe not. This certainly was not the workout she had intended for today.

Up she went, higher, faster—what a ride. Nothing like this at the amusement park, that's for sure. Nikki thought she would explode—she had to. No one could survive this—and in a sauna, of all places! Thank God the temperature wasn't two hundred degrees.

Both women were dripping wet everywhere—sweat mixed with come—both bodies glowed red in the heat of the sauna and the heat of the moment. Nikki arched her body up into the woman's face, her hands grasping her shoulders, head—here it came, the uncontrollable spasms, shaking, juice flowing out like a thick, creamy river. Nikki couldn't get any air—how long could you be in a sauna before you passed out? At last she collapsed on the bench, the woman's head resting between her legs. She withdrew her hand and moved gently up towards Nikki. "There's something I forgot to mention," the woman said. Opening her eyes, Nikki came face to face with this woman who had given her such pleasure. The woman leaned down and kissed Nikki very softly. "Remember when I said my husband liked other women?"

"Yes," replied Nikki.

"Well, I forgot to tell you that I like other women, too."

"Really?" said Nikki, smiling at the joke. "I had no idea. You sure hide it well."

To which the woman replied, "See you around the weight room?"

"Same time tomorrow."

"Good deal."

"I don't even know your name. My name's—"

Before Nikki had a chance to finish, the woman placed a hand over her mouth. "Let's leave it this way. More mystery, don't you agree? Besides, I don't need to know your name to know that I like making love to you. You'll see me again. Next time will be your turn."

She got up, wrapped her towel around her waist, looked back at Nikki with a smile, opened the door and left. Nikki sat there soaked, exhausted, feeling the heat. She started to get up, reaching for her towel when she heard the door open and heard a voice: "Mind if I join you?"

Nikki thought—another two minutes. What can it hurt?

Veronica and Roses

I was rapidly discovering that life on the other side of the fence wasn't all we working grunts thought it was. And the other side of the fence I'm talking about is being part of MANAGEMENT, as opposed to THE REST OF THE WORKING JOES (a.k.a. the PROLETARIAT). Ever since that night when Don (my boss) informed me I was moving up the corporate ladder I had wondered whether it was such a wise decision on my part to accept it. Maybe I was just having trouble negotiating the rungs of the ladder, I don't know. I hadn't tripped yet. But I found myself putting in more time at the office than I ever dreamed was humanly possible. And no overtime! At least as a grunt I got time and a half.

And meetings...ughhh, meetings. Every Monday morning, 8:00 A.M. Sure made it hard to tie one on at the local women's bar on Sunday night, that's for sure. Meetings with all the usual management acronyms— AD (Art Director), CD (Creative Director—that was me!), VP, Senior VP, Executive VP—no P, though. We never saw Jacob Stark, the company's founder and president. Maybe he knew something about meetings that we didn't. Lucky guy. Sometimes we would have meetings to plan meetings. But most of the time our meetings would be real snoozers until someone pulled what I like to call a "voice mail"—a forty-five minute discussion about some topic that had no resolution, like the pros and cons of voice mail. Then I would wake up and get angry that the meeting was being prolonged by such an idiot. Uggh...meetings.

Sadly, the worst thing about my new position was the lack of time I got to spend with Karen. You remember Karen Myers, right? Downstairs at the engineering firm. We had an adventure on my drafting table...and in my bed later that night...sigh. Over the course of the last four months we were making some nice progress with developing a relationship, but this management thing had put a major cramp in it. I hadn't had a night free to spend with her for two weeks! And the one night I did spend at her place, we had a nice hot bath, some wine and I fell asleep at 8:00. She was very sweet about it the next morning, but lately I've heard this distinctive edge in her voice when we talk on the phone. Of course, we never meet at the copier anymore—I have a secretary who does all my copying. She even fixes the copier—I was not Ms. Fixit anymore. So our relationship had progressed from handcuffed ecstasy on the table to sawing off a lamp to stilted phone conversations. What was next? Pie in the face? Probably.

"Chris, call on line two," Alex, my secretary's voice crackled through the speaker. I have told Alex time after time to tell me who is on the phone, in case I want to screen them out. She's nice, efficient and makes great coffee. But she has her own agenda....

So I picked up the phone and said, "Chris Munoz."

"Hi sweetie." It was Karen.

"Hi. How are you?" I hadn't talked to her since yesterday.

"Okay, I guess. Are you available tomorrow night? Thought we could go downtown and check out that new movie *Chained Heat III*. Then dinner at...say that Afghan restaurant?" Karen had a knack for finding little, out of the way Third World places to eat. Last month it was an Ethiopian restaurant....

"I'm sorry, I wish I could but I've got this management conference to go to at the Guest Quarters. I told you about it last time we talked."

"Well, then maybe Thursday night?"

"It's a three day conference. I'll be back Friday afternoon. Maybe we could do something that night."

"Yeah, and you'll be asleep by the time the movie's over." Karen's voice had a harsher edge to it now, bordering on sarcasm.

"How do you know that?" I threw up the shield to ward off any more blows. "I can still hang. I'm not that old yet. And have you seen the reviews for *Chained Heat III*? They say Brigitte Nielsen's acting is a step down from Sylvester Stallone on downers."

"Yeah, which means she'll be more fun to watch than you." Oooh, we have now crossed the border and we've gone into heavy, biting sarcasm.

"Look, Karen, I don't think this is doing us any good. Why don't I call you back tonight when I can talk?" Just then, Alex's voice seared through my eardrums. "Chris, Mr. Walker is on three and he's in his car." Mr. Walker was Don, my boss. And calling from the car meant that he was not in the mood to waste dollars on his car phone. I had to go. Now.

"Karen, I have to go. It's Don and he's in the car. I'll call you later, okay?"

"Don't bother, I won't be home."

"Well, I'll leave a message, okay?"

"Leave a message. I won't promise that I'll listen to it." Boy, she was pissed. I said my good-bye and then punched line three and listened to Don telling me what additional slides he wanted me to prepare for the conference. "Just do it in Director (which is the name of a multi-media presentation program for Macintosh), and leave the disk on my desk. I'll see you at the hotel at 8:00 sharp."

I sighed as I hung up. It was now 3:00. I had to finish a report, look over some printing estimates, work up the specs for pocket folders for a local hospital, and create six new slides for Don. And then be at the Guest Quarters by 8:00 tomorrow morning, bright eyed and bushy tailed.

As the sky turned a muted shade of orange and purple, I worked furiously trying to get everything together. Being so busy helped take my mind off of Karen temporarily, but I knew that I couldn't keep sweeping this under the carpet. Eventually I'd have to decide if I was really serious about seeing her. Because if I was serious, then I'd have to make the effort. Management or no management.

I arrived home about 7:30, grabbed a Dos Equis and some cold shrimp fried rice from the fridge, collapsed on the couch watching CNN and listening to my answering machine. As expected, Karen hadn't left me a message. Everyone else had, including my mother asking if I'd met any nice boys yet. I had told my mother at least five hundred times that I was gay and every time she'd roll her eyes upward and say, "Oh, you just haven't met the right man yet." She was in permanent denial, I guess. I called everyone back (except my mother), took a shower, set the alarm for 5:30 and went to bed. I'd get my clothes together in the morning. I was so exhausted....

5:30 A.M...oh, mannn, why didn't I pack last night? I could've slept till at least 7:00. In my bleary-eyed stupor I swung my feet over the edge of my platform bed, stood up and started for the bathroom. When I'm this tired, a shower is usually the first thing I need just to get awake enough to make coffee.

Still struggling to open my eyes, I turned the water on, pulled the shower handle and stepped in…to freezing cold water! Where was the hot water? I kept turning the hot water handle up and turning the cold down, yet nothing was happening. Disgusted, I turned everything off and got out of the shower. My first management conference and I was going to be dirty. Thinking about having to call the landlady and complain wasn't making me feel any better. I have got to save some money and buy a house. That way, all the problems are mine and mine alone…but then they'll get fixed in a hurry.

Well, in a pinch baby powder would have to do, so I hit the bottle heavily, with an extra dose in my underwear, and started to get dressed. I had exactly one work outfit left that didn't look like it had been slept in. A quick ironing session was next….

Packed and ready to go. I hadn't even bothered with coffee, as distracted as I was by the lack of hot water. I could pick some up on the way. I checked my briefcase, making sure I had all my essentials. Ready or not, here I come.

The trip to the hotel was uneventful, save for the local 7-Eleven where I was unable to purchase any freshly brewed coffee—this stuff was awful. I was rattled when I arrived, frantic for some java and in a total panic about my slides. I had left the disk with Don, and he was not the most computer-literate man in the world. Miraculously, the morning part of the meeting went without a hitch—my slides were very well received— and in the proper order! As we broke for lunch, a hotel desk clerk came up, placed a folded piece of paper in my hand and said, "This person called for you. She said she had an appointment with you and asked for your room number. We can't give the room number without permission. She said she'd call back in an hour."

Puzzled, I unfolded the paper and somehow made out the name "Veronica" scrawled in the clerk's nearly unin- telligible scribble. Veronica who? As I continued to stare at the note, I managed to make out parts of a phrase, "has what you need." "Did she say this…has what I need?" I queried the clerk. The clerk nodded affirma- tively and I was baffled even further. And then my mind, ever in search of the next bad thing to think about, started imagining what Veronica might be like. Tall. Leggy. Blonde. Nothing at all like Karen, even though I found Karen very attractive. Blondes were my downfall.

"When she calls, shall I give out the room number?"

"Absolutely," I replied, almost without hesitation. I was now captured by wild thoughts of Veronica, and I wasn't going to waste an opportunity to see what she was all about. Even if she was straight, she was probably worth a look or two.

The rest of the day's meeting was a complete blur as I continued to fantasize about this mystery woman who wanted my room number. Who had I told about my being here? Karen knew, but this was not Karen. Especially after I saw how angry she was with me. Everyone at work knew, of course. Could this be someone at work, playing a little joke on the token dyke? Well, this would certainly be fun….

I stopped at the front desk after the meeting broke up and asked for messages. There weren't any. I was a little disappointed that Miss Veronica hadn't left a message. I was also a little dismayed that Karen hadn't called. Maybe I should call her after dinner.

Don had asked if I would join him and Ron (my other boss) for dinner in the hotel restaurant. I had politely declined, publicly declaring my extreme desire to have a bath, room service and fall asleep. But I was full of energy, ready and raring to go. And no Miss Veronica. Oh well. I opened the door to my room, flipped on the light switch and was stunned by the dozen red roses lying on one of the beds. I sat on the bed, picked one rose up and inhaled the sweet fragrance. There was no card, note, nothing. Thoroughly confused, I was jolted out of my daze by the phone. The mystery florist? I picked up the receiver, said hello, and heard: "This is the front desk. I have a message for you. Veronica asked that you meet her in the bar at 7:00."

These had to be…Veronica? How did she get in my room? Maybe she bribed the maid. My curiosity was at full tilt now. The clock said 6:00. I had time…too much time. Maybe I should call Karen now. I dialed nine to get out, then dialed her number. As I expected, I got her machine. I left what I thought was a fairly nice message—not too groveling, not too distant, just right. Maybe she was so fed up she went out with someone... and then I started to feel a little guilty. Here I am, meeting a woman I don't even know, have never even seen, having dinner with her...and that's all it would be, I was sure. Time to snap out of the dream. She was probably straight, someone I knew from work playing a joke on me. Well, I could just laugh it off, have fun with it. And then I could get serious about Karen. Time for a shower...a nice, *hot* shower...with nice, *hot* water....

I dressed in my semi-dyke best, which for me is white T-shirt, black vest, and baggy Dockers. I threw in my favorite old scuffed pair of Doc Martens for added effect. Add a thumb ring, ear cuff, and rainbow rings, and I was a flaming advertisement for the Isle of Lesbos. Well, at least I wasn't hiding anything.

I made it to the bar about ten of seven, which is a bad sign. Never be the first one there. Well, I could kill some time with a beer, so I hit the barkeep for a Guiness Stout and turned my attention to the trivia game which was right next to me. How convenient. I sat and played some sports trivia...and won. Then I played some sex trivia...and lost. Not a good sign. After about 10 minutes I was becoming bored and I kept looking at my watch. 7:00, then 7:15. I ordered another Guiness, then the thought hit me: how do I know what Veronica looks like? I wouldn't even know if she was in the room. She obviously must know what I look like. I was not going to come out a winner at all. I scanned the room—there was one woman in the room besides me and she was with two guys in a booth. Odds are that this was not her.

The hour passed and I got a little more sloshed. About 8:15 I was hungry, drunk, tired and fed up. I was wasting my time here, and I couldn't afford to get totally wasted, not with more meetings tomorrow. So I paid my check, told the bartender to tell Veronica to shove it (if she ever arrived) and left.

As the elevator whooshed up to the fifth floor, I couldn't help but feel very stupid. Suddenly, the last bit of adrenaline drained out of me and I felt like a wet dishcloth. At least I would get a good night's sleep, what with all the beer and being as tired as I was feeling. I put my keycard in the door, opened the door and flicked on the light switch. Nothing. Burnt out bulb? I felt my way along the wall, remembering that there was a desk lamp on the dresser and cursing myself for not remembering how big the dresser was as the sharp edge drove into my knee and I howled in pain.

Being in total darkness, I was reluctant to prance around the room holding my knee, so I wisely stayed my ground and searched for the desk lamp. Ahhh, found it. Found the little toggle switch...nothing. Was there a power outage? But the hall lights had been on. Maybe there was a power outage in...my room? I looked around in the blackness and my eyes focused on the red l.e.d. numbers of the alarm clock. The alarm was working. Just the lights.

And then I heard a sound, just the slightest sound like cloth rustling. As my eyes grew accustomed to the blackness, I tried to make out the room. I couldn't really see anything except the alarm clock. Was someone in here with me? Gingerly moving, I attempted to find the bed and was successful. I sat down on the edge and tried to think clearly, which is difficult when you've got a load on. And then a hand touched my shoulder. I nearly screamed, then I felt something cool, soft and sweet smelling touch my shoulder...a rose. This had to be...Veronica?

Whoever it was smelled wonderful and her hands were all over me almost instantly. Being in such a Guiness-weakened state as I was, I put up very little resistance to her ministrations. Thoughts of Karen quickly dissipated as I succumbed to the evil, delicious spell woven by Miss X. Wordlessly she worked her black magic as she undid my belt, and I felt her hands plunge into my pants, taking their time and exploring every part of me. Thank god for that nice, *hot*, hotel shower....

I started to do a little exploring of my own, but she resisted me. She leaned into me, forcing me to lie down on the bed. She turned me over onto my stomach, and started massaging my back. Ahhh, maybe this wasn't going to be what I thought it would be. But this was just as nice, in a way...then I felt her hands on my arms, moving them, until they were behind my back. And then the shock of cold steel clasped around my wrists— handcuffs—handcuffed behind my back. She was definitely a pro, massaging me into oblivion and then going for the kill.

Then she went to work, turning me over and her lips were everywhere—on my lips, neck, ears, breasts. While her lips were busy, her hands played with my nipples, caressing and pinching, and driving me into a frenzy I had not known since that first night with Karen. Oops, don't think about her right now. Focus on the here and now.

The room was still enveloped in black, as if a black drape had been hung. I couldn't see a thing, and wasn't particularly caring. Miss X moved her very active tongue further down my torso until she found what she and I were hoping she would find. I was very, very ready. And then I felt the familiar hard plastic of old reliable Ms. Vibrator sneaking into my cunt. She flicked it on and then moved it over my clit, up and down, side to side...then I heard the buzz stop and felt her tongue back again. And she really went to work, licking, sucking, penetrating—I was positive the bed was becoming soaked with me. I could feel a big one coming and I rode it as long as I could until the dam broke and I whispered, "No more."

Everything feels so good when it's over. I can't explain it and I'm sure none of us can. But the expression "slept like a baby" generally describes the wonderful kind of sleep one usually has after such a satisfying, exhausting sexual encounter. I heard the door click open as Miss X left. I didn't even bother to ask about the lights, I was in such sweet oblivion. And then I fell asleep....

And woke to the sound of the phone ringing at 6 A.M.
A wake up call. I tried to move my arms to answer it,
and to my horror discovered that I was still handcuffed!
Oh boy this pile was getting deeper and deeper. I
managed to get myself on my feet, the sunlight straining
to come in through the drawn drapes. At least it was
morning and I could see better. I racked my brain trying
to think while my feet mindlessly moved me toward the
dresser. And then I saw a red rose. Underneath the rose
was a note with a tiny silver thing attached. The key!
The note said, *Thought you might need this. Last night was
fun. Let's do it again—Love, V.* I had to stand at the dresser
backwards so that my fingers could grasp the handcuff
key. Fortunately the dresser was waist high. I would
have been in trouble if it had been eye level.

Freed from my manacles, I showered and got dressed,
the thought occurring to me that I hadn't asked for a
wake up call. That Miss X. She sure was on top of things.
If it hadn't been for her, I would've been late for my
meeting. And if it hadn't been for her...well, never mind.

After the day's meetings were concluded, Don said to
me, "There's no reason for you to stay tonight if you
don't want to. Tomorrow is a very short meeting that
really doesn't involve you and then we play golf. Unless
you want to hang with us and play bad golf, you may as
well check out and head for home. Thanks for all your
hard work. You really made an impression."

Yeah, Don, I guess I made an impression on someone,
not to mention blowing out all the light bulbs in my room

with a total stranger. I thanked him for the compliment and made plans to get out and head for home. I called Karen again from the room but hung up before the machine could pick up. This was not going well. In my euphoria from the night before, I had neglected to think about how badly things really were getting with Karen. We'd have to talk. Maybe it was better if we didn't see each other for a while. Then again, there was Miss X—Veronica. If only I had gotten her number, or her real name....

While on the freeway, I decided to stop off at Karen's apartment. It was early, and she wouldn't be home yet. But I had a key and could wait for her. Then we could talk. After I entered her apartment, I sat down, turned on the TV and watched the Comedy Channel. The phone rang and I started for the kitchen to answer it, then remembered the answering machine would get it. Besides, what if it was someone I didn't know...like the woman she went out with last night? I waited in the hallway for the machine to kick in, heard the "beep" and then heard a very faggy guy's voice say, "Hey Karrie (her friends called her Karrie), howya doing? Hope the roses did the trick. Let's get together and do some dancing sometime, okay? Eddie's really missin' you." Then he hung up. I wondered who Mr. Fag was and who Eddie was—probably Mr. Fag's lover...what roses?

I looked all over the living room and kitchen, searching for roses. I went into the bedroom and turned on the light. Except the light didn't go on. I checked the plug, then looked in the lamp. No light bulb. Maybe she had forgotten to replace it. I walked over to the other night-stand and turned on the light. Nothing. Same thing—no bulb. Then I heard a key in the door and the door open. I walked out of the bedroom and saw Karen, who jumped when she saw me.

"What are you doing here?"

"Waiting for you. I thought we should talk, but maybe we don't have to after all."

"I'm still mad at you."

"You have a funny way of showing it. You need light bulbs."

"What?"

"I waited for you in the bar, Veronica. Thanks for not showing up."

"I was busy. What are you talking about, the bar?"

"I've got it figured out, Karen. The light bulbs were for practice. And thanks for the wake-up call. But a double thanks for the handcuff key. I guess you went and bought some new handcuffs after that last episode we had. But the real giveaway was your fag friend who left you the message on your machine about the roses."

"Oh, that's Bernie. He and Eddie were my first roommates."

"He does nice work. The roses were beautiful. And so were you...now could I have my turn, please?"

And with that, my arms were around her and we went off to the bedroom, in search of a reprise between Veronica and me...with a working pair of handcuffs, no light bulbs and a desire that was seemingly unquenchable....

What If

It's fun to imagine. Everybody should devote at least one hour in each day to do nothing except let their mind wander. No reading the paper, no watching the crap on TV, not even listening to music. No external stimulation except what's within. Just close your eyes, lie down or sit yoga-style, however you prefer, and just imagine....

We are in her house. She invited me over for dinner. We are friends, but lately we have both acknowledged that there is some attraction between us. As I sit at her kitchen table watching her prepare a salad, my right leg twitches in anticipation. Anticipation of what? Maybe

I'm thinking that tonight we'll do more than talk. Maybe I'm planning what I'm going to say to her, the exact words to get her into my arms, and when I take her face in my hands, that exquisitely crafted face, and my lips travel across her face, searching for their counterparts....

"Do you like cucumbers?" she says.

I tell her yes, I love cucumbers, and she continues cutting, the sound of the knife *whomp* as it hits the cutting board again and again. I love to watch her. I could sit here all night and just gaze, my eyes taking in her hair, down her back, her legs, the way she stands, moves across the floor to open the refrigerator. All so fluid, the movements. Like the ocean waves, the rolling movements, the way each wave is perfect in form. That's her. Perfection in my eyes.

Dinner is marvelous I suppose, because I cannot remember what I've eaten. We have talked and consumed one bottle of wine and are on our second, but it's not the wine that's impaired my mental faculties. It's her. It's her voice, the sound of her laughter, the way her hand moves when she draws on her cigarette. She takes another cigarette from the pack and places it between her lips. I halfway stand, grasp her lighter before she can get to it. She looks at me with that funny little smile that turns her mouth just slightly higher on one side than the other. As I lean over to light her cigarette, I am still staring at her smile and all of a sudden I hear a sound (what's that?), and as I look away from her I see that I've struck my wine glass and the wine has spilled onto the tablecloth, now it's dripping onto the hardwood floor. What a klutz! Oh man, I hope she's not mad at me. Quickly I run to the kitchen for some towels. She is already bending down and wiping the floor with her napkin. "At least it's not red wine," I hear myself say along with the clumsy, "I'm sorry." She looks up at me and tells me it's okay. I bend down and curse my prematurely arthritic knees as I drop to the floor and apply my towels to the mop up.

It looks dry. I raise my head and as I do so our eyes align. This must be an out-of-body experience, because what is happening could not be happening to me. I must be a spectator watching someone else's fingers reach for her hair. But it feels real. Her hair on my fingers. So soft, as I knew it would be. My hands move from her hair to her face, to caress, to explore as though I were blind and needed to feel every inch of her to know her. I have this awful lump in my throat—it must be cancer or something because I can't speak! Well, if it's terminal then what the hell—let's go for broke. Who cares about tomorrow? So I try to speak and all I can manage is, "You're so beautiful." So mundane. The lump reappears in my throat. I don't think I'll say another word until I can come up with better lines. Where's the script for something like this? I am not prepared at all.

But miraculously she hasn't seemed to notice my vocabulary deficiency. Or maybe it's happening to her too. Anyway, her hand reaches up and grasps my hand and our fingers interlock. I raise her hand to my lips and softly kiss her fingers, the back of her hand, run my tongue lightly across her palm. It is now that I notice my hand shaking just slightly. I am definitely not prepared at all. I look her in the eye (I have such trouble with direct eye contact), and I put my arms around her and draw her into me. A hug feels good right now because I am shaken and I don't know what to do next. I mean, it's not as though I haven't thought about a night like this, but it's always different in dreams and imagination. Everything moves in slow motion so each move is always easy to plan and execute. Now it's real and it's moving too fast. I need to slow the film down.

The hug is working; her body eases into mine. It's as though we fit together like some interlocking puzzle. This hug is different from the ones we normally have when we say good-bye…this is developing a rhythm, a rocking movement. Our hands are probing each other, moving up and down our spines, across shoulders, fingers dig into muscle, kneading, grasping….

There are many events that have happened in my life of which I cannot always remember every detail. With the passage of time, images lose their crispness, words become garbled. I can say that there are very few events which keep their original clarity, their brightness, cleanness, their virginity, which exist as the master print from which all second generation copies are made, like the original master tape the musician makes in the studio or the original painting from which subsequent numbered prints are made. The events that happened next are stored in that gilded vault in my mind in which original masters reside.

I feel her arms loosen and I step back just slightly. My hands reach out; one around the back of her neck, the other touches her face. I can feel myself leaning in toward her, and before I know it my lips are touching hers. Gliding across, at first lightly, afraid if I ask for too much she will pull away. I always tell myself that if she should reject me I will understand, but tonight I feel a quiet desperation as I kiss her, knowing that if she should pull away I will be devastated, inconsolable. Again, this is all happening too fast—we need slow motion in real life. But she does not pull away; her lips are responding to mine. Slowly, at first, but I can feel her growing stronger, more sure of herself.

My lips move across her face, behind her ear (I have thought about those ears!), then down her neck. My hands move from her face, to her shoulders, to her waist. I purposely avoid her upper body—I still think this must be a dream and surely I will awaken at any minute. Her hands are on my waist and her arms wrap around me. I suddenly regret the last glass of wine—am I too far gone? Will I remember all of this? Please, God, help me remember every moment. But since this must be a dream, I guess I can do whatever I want and not suffer consequences, since I will eventually wake up. Well, here goes. My hands travel up her body until I feel it change. Her breasts are small—that is easily discernible from sight alone. But I am now touching them through the fabric. My fingers slide up, over, around, feeling the nipples growing taut. What's that? I heard a sound...a small sigh escaped from her lips. She likes it! She wants me! Absolutely incredible. I can't believe it. This dream is really something.

We continue to kiss, lips parted and tongues exploring, and then I feel something new: her hands on my body. Tracing my hips, my waist, running up my torso until they reach my breasts. Ohh, man, what am I gonna do now? runs through my head. It's impossible to think, all I can do is react, and I hear sounds resonate through my body. My legs are not stable; the expression "legs turn to jelly" definitely applies. I actually might faint. Oh God, what if I faint, or burp, throw up, something else awful (what could be more awful than the afore-mentioned)? Just when I've imagined every possible romantic disaster, I hear her say, "I love the way you feel," and my attention is diverted (thankfully!) back to reality. Or the dream I'm having that seems to be reality. Whatever. Now my hands reach down to her pants, pulling fabric until I can move my hands underneath her shirt. Now we're happening. Fingers on skin. Flesh on flesh. Brassiere? Merely a small impediment. We move it up and out of the way and now we've got what we came for. Ahhh, smooth skin, round mound of flesh that my hand easily can cover, with that fascinating tip which stays hard between my fingers. Moving my fingers back and forth, back and forth, up and down, crossing the top, I can hear more sighs, feel her body move against me.

Okay, let's move. Fingers undo the clasp that holds this brassiere contraption together. Buttons undone rapidly, and all of a sudden her naked torso is within view. Oh, and she's so…God, I've got that lump in my throat again. Beautiful? No, that's not right. Too common. Exquisite? I've used that before in this story. But she is. Exquisite. Delicate. So…I don't know, I can't say, I might cry. Cry? I know there's no crying in baseball, but what about sex scenes? So…

I stifle the urge to cry by covering her breast with my lips. Moving gently at first, circling the tip with my tongue, running my tongue over and over, feeling her breast moving with each flick of my tongue, up and down. This was a good move, I can tell. So now what? The shirt is history; I ask her if she wants to go somewhere else more comfortable (we have been standing in the dining room all this time!). She takes my hand and I follow her upstairs, turning the corner at the top, and we go into her bedroom. The bed is high; I'm short. She sits on the bed; I kneel before her and my face barely comes up to her waist. Not a problem. I undo her pants, zipper comes down, I'm kissing her, following the trail of the zipper as it moves downward. I place my hands on her thighs, moving up to her hips and I gently move her onto the bed lying down. Wow, is this really happening? Dream is still on. Okay…I sit straddling her, her pants coming down, she starts pulling my clothes, shirt coming up, up, over my head, there it's off, now it's her hands on my naked flesh, playing, moving, my nipples between her fingers. Ohh, something's gonna happen if I don't—if I don't what? If I don't take control, that's what. No, this one is mine. Then you can play with me if you want to.

So, newly fortified with a slightly butchy attitude, I move in. On top, lying down, pressing myself against her. With both hands I pin her arms against the pillow over her head (no tying knots with white scarves—this is not Basic Instinct). Just so I can concentrate. As I hold her arms, my head moves, trailing kisses down her body, her neck, breasts—I love those and pay special attention—all the way way down, down—oops, underwear. No time for those. Pull 'em down, off. Yes, there we are. Ohh, what a sight. She's even more beautiful than I imagined, or could imagine. Kissing her everywhere, moving down her belly, down, down, until I find her legs over my ears, around my head, my tongue flicking out to taste her, she is so sweet. I savor every drop of her. I want more. I keep tasting, rolling my tongue, pushing it against the spot that makes her jump. She arches into me, pushing gently against my mouth. I'm going faster now, taking everything she's giving me. She is flowing into me, into my mouth, faster, coming at me faster, come on, come on, I've got you now, just a little more, we're almost there….

Imagination…sigh. How wonderful.

While the Wash Turns

Well, things are looking up for me. I think you know me—I'm Kate, the one with the nice fat black eye in "The Shiner" (if you don't know me, read the story). I got taken out by Big Jean at the local lesbo hangout and, just when the dark clouds were threatening to break open, an angel appeared with ice in a towel—the angel Mary.

And you may recall that Mary drove me home without knowing how to drive stick. She fixed my eye and wrecked my alignment, and by the end of the weekend she moved in and I was in love. We never got out of bed until Monday morning when that nasty thing called work came calling. This work thing is playing havoc with our new thing which has been going on for six months now. We're like two shifts passing in the night—just when I'm dragging in the door at 6:00, she's on her way out to do the night shift at the Savoy Diner. At least we both get the weekends off and we spend them in bed. Not sleeping, mind you. I am getting used to binging on sex during the weekend, and abstaining during the week—sort of a sexual bulimic, I guess.

As I said, things are looking up. We moved out of my little third floor apartment into a real house. Just renting, though. We'd like to buy someday. Yes, things are getting better. We have a little yard with a fence. Mary has a garden where she's experimenting with some sort of hybrid monster cucumbers. We're just like every other married couple. During the week, I'm so beat from work I usually just crash in front of the TV with whatever wonderful meal Mary cooks and leaves for me to microwave. Sometimes she leaves me a note asking me to do something for her like laundry. She leaves me notes all over the place, come to think of it. Just like Felix Unger.

So when I came home from work at 6:30 Tuesday night, I was very surprised to see Mary's car in front of the house and Mary sitting on the front steps crying. "It's been a bad day, Kate," she sobbed as I kissed her. "First the coffee-maker broke. I skipped aerobics to wait for the cable guy and he never showed up." (Our reception was awful and I had been threatening to storm the cable office like a postal worker.) "And then the washer broke. Just stopped right in the middle of the rinse cycle. The repair man's answering service said he'd call later tonight. And now my car won't start! I'm just too stressed out to go to work so I called in sick." Mary sat back down on the steps with an unhappy sigh, her brow furrowed like a freshly plowed field. I plopped down next to her and heaved a big sigh of my own. Everything was a disaster. Especially no coffee maker. We were big into coffee.

Quickly I put on my smooth-things-out cap. "Well, let's think this all through. Coffee maker's not a problem. I'll get another one tomorrow after work. We can make do with Dunkin' Donuts for now."

"What about my car?" Mary wailed. Not being very mechanical, I was at a loss to ascertain the possible reasons for it not starting. "I know—I'll call Weezie," (she was one of the dykes I hung out with B.M.—Before Mary). "She's into cars—works on them, changes oil and stuff. Maybe she could come over and take a look at it. If not, we'll break down and call Triple A to come tow it to the Sunoco a couple of blocks up. If I get out of work on time tomorrow night, I can drive you to work. Maybe you could get a ride home."

Mary's calmer demeanor suggested that I was on the right track, so I continued. "The cable? I'm so fed up with them I'm ready to cancel and buy a satellite dish, except the washer is probably more important right now.

It's old and we've spent a fortune on it just in the last 3 months. We'll just have to splurge and buy a new one, I guess. As far as the load that's in the machine, why don't we pile it all up and go to the Laundromat?"

The Laundromat. I can't even believe I suggested it. I have not been to a Laundromat since I was in college. I remember many a midnight hour struck while I was plunking twenty-five cents in the detergent vending machine. The aroma of hot wet clothes. Sitting on those plastic chairs doing a term paper while the drunk frat boys stumbled by outside, stopping to take a piss at the front window. What fond memories I have of Laundromats.

Mary brightened up immediately. "Yeah, the Laundromat! Why didn't I think of that? You know—" She suddenly stood up and pulled me up with her, "—at least we'll be spending some time together tonight."

At the Laundromat, the new hot place to meet. Right.

We went inside. I changed my clothes, got out of my work togs and into my going-to-the-laundromat attire, which I remembered from college as a torn sweat shirt and cut offs. Mary was down in the basement taking the wet load out. I placed a quick call to Weezie, who chastised me up and down for being invisible of late, then immediately agreed to come over and look at the car if I would leave her a six-pack of Bud.

Mary and I got our things together for our laundry date. I packed a copy of *Rubyfruit Jungle* to reread for the thousandth time. She had her back turned so I didn't see what she was doing. I saw the strap of her backpack and I assumed she was packing her own reading material. As we left the house I placed the Bud, wrapped in a plastic bag with some ice, and Mary's car keys inside the screen door, and we were off for the land of suds and duds. Suddenly I wished I was Weezie, staying at home to get all greasy working on the car, drinking my Bud and burping like Weezie. Just one of the guys....

The Laundromat was located in a small shopping center with a drugstore and pizzeria as neighbors. Here we come, the intrepid washer-women, pulling into the parking lot, my tires squealing loudly. Thelma and Louise we weren't. Once inside, I took notice of our other washerly neighbors and realized that I probably wasn't going to run into any of my old frat buddies. It was 7:30 at night, and most of the clientele were women—straight women I assumed. They all had that look—the 'I've got three little rug rats at home who are driving me crazy so get out of my way' look. As I glanced at what they were taking out of the dryer, I knew I had guessed correctly—men's underwear, little kids' socks, shirts and pants, etc. I wondered what Mary and I had in the laundry bag.

Mary took care of getting the load into the washer. I settled into a plastic chair and started to review *Rubyfruit Jungle*—still one of my all-time favorites. I especially love the episode with the grapefruit. I was starting to get into the book, which means I am getting lost to civilization, when a shadow fell over the pages.

"I have to wash it all over again, which should take about 30 minutes. You wanna go over to the pizza shop and get some coffee?" Mary's brown eyes danced with a wickedness I did not recall ever seeing. Something was up with her.

"Sure," I agreed, getting up and following her outside, taking *Rubyfruit* with me.

I was headed for the pizza shop when Mary's hand tugged at my arm. "I have a better idea," she said. I started to say something but she put a hand over my mouth. "Just follow me, honey. This will be fun, I promise."

Wordlessly I obeyed, she leading me by the hand. We walked toward the end of the shopping center, turned right, and we headed toward the back of the center. Mary had her backpack slung over her shoulder. Something was clinking inside. I was becoming intrigued by the mysterious contents of the bag.

We stopped just outside the back of the Laundromat. The parking lot ended and there was nothing but woods behind us. The air smelled of dryer exhaust. How romantic.

"I thought since we had an unexpected night together, we should celebrate," Mary said as she unearthed two wine glasses from her bag, handing one to me. She removed a nice bottle of white wine and a corkscrew, deftly pulled the cork out and poured the wine as I looked admiringly at her. She really was an angel—with a devil's eye.

We sat down on the back step of the laundromat, sipping our wine and holding hands. Her head rested on my shoulder, and then her lips moved to my neck. At this point, I was not noticing the stinky dryer exhaust anymore—nothing else seemed very important except the fact that we were having an intimate moment on a weeknight. We kissed for what seemed like an hour and then we both set our wine glasses down and set our hands to work. Hers were inside my sweatshirt and on my nipples. My hands were unbuttoning her shirt, then I moved down and started sucking on her breasts. For a moment I had this thought that they tasted different on a weeknight than on a weekend.

Things were progressing very nicely when suddenly the atmosphere was pierced by an obnoxious beeping sound.

"Oh, no, I'll be right back." Mary stood up, turning off the alarm in her wristwatch and buttoning her shirt.

"What's going on?" I demanded.

"The wash. I've got to unload the washer and put the clothes in the dryer," Mary said as she ran off and disappeared around the corner. I was left sulking on the step. Sulking can be a marvelous thing to do—if you get on the proper high horse, you can do it all day. I did not want to be too moody since the evening had started out with such promise. I decided the next best thing to do would be to drink wine, so I did. I poured myself a glass and guzzled it. Whoa, horsie. That hit the spot. Mary wasn't back yet, so I poured another glass and drank it a little bit slower than the first one—by about three seconds. Factor in the lack of anything substantial in my stomach and you can guess that I was very buzzed right about then.

I stood up, or tried to. I wasn't very successful. I decided to try to walk and I made it as far as the end of the parking lot, where I collapsed on the grass under a nice fat oak tree. I laid down, gazing up at the now-dark summer sky. Mmmm, this is nice. My eyes closed and I was buzzing off somewhere, lost in the rinse cycle. Something was tickling me—couldn't be a bug, this felt much nicer. And this bug or whatever it was had lips. I opened my eyes and Mary was on top of me, her lips on my breasts, licking and sucking. Holy ring around the collar. I was getting molested by the laundry woman.

She unzipped my cut-offs and yanked them down to my ankles. I tore at her shirt, several buttons coming off in the process. She pulled the drawstring loose on her sweatpants and I did the rest, my hands exploring her cunt along the way. We were nearly naked, lying in the grass, one big sixty-nine under the old oak tree. Her tongue ran over my clit, licking, then sucking, harder and harder. My mouth was full of her, my tongue ran inside, tasting her juices which were freely flowing. Both of us were furiously licking and sucking each other and I felt the spring tighten up inside and get ready to uncoil in a big way.

Just when I thought I might have reached the jumping off point, Mary surprised me again, in a very pleasant way. I felt something hard and smooth enter me, exit and then enter again. She kept this up while her tongue continued to massage my clit. I did my best to reciprocate, thrusting my fingers into her and licking her. We kept this going for a short while, and then I hit the wall—slammed into it and slid down, is more like it. All those weekends of non-stop sex and here I was coming like no tomorrow outside of the Laundromat.

I was so wrapped up in my own coming I didn't notice if Mary had her own, but she let out a huge sigh that was her signal to me that she had indeed hit the same wall I had. We lay together in the grass for a few minutes. The sound of voices in the distance roused us from our splendid stupor, so we quickly got ourselves together, stood up and walked back to the back of the laundromat to reclaim our things. Mary's shirt was missing several buttons, which I pointed out to her.

"I'll just take one of the sweatshirts out of the dryer," she said.

Wash. It dawned on me why we had come in the first place. I now had new fond memories of Laundromats.

We went around to the front and into the Laundromat. The wash was done. I helped fold, we took everything out to the car and drove home, snuggled up together in the front seat. The happy threesome—two dykes and their laundry.

Just as we pulled up, Weezie was getting into her pickup. "The distributor cap was cracked. I put a second-hand one on I had lying around in the truck here, and it's okay for now. When it's light out I'll put a new one on. Cost ya about ten dollars, I figure. I cleaned the plugs, too. They were a little dirty, but they're okay. Should last a while. Thanks for the brewski. Gotta go—wife's waitin', ya know what I mean?" Weezie was kind of like a man. She tossed us the keys and drove off.

We went into the house, I grabbed the remote and clicked on the TV. Same old snowy cable. Well, two out of three ain't bad, right?

"So maybe we'll go look for a washer over the week-end, okay?" Mary said as she walked up the stairs with the laundry basket.

"What for? I think I kind of like the Laundromat now," I replied as I ran up the stairs behind her, my hand grabbing her ass. "I see you've been in my bottom drawer. Which one was it—the black beauty?" I kept all my toys in the bottom right hand drawer of the dresser. The black vibrator with the gold tip was my favorite.

Mary laughed and said, "No, I haven't been in the drawer."

"Then where'd you get it?"

"It wasn't a vibrator."

"A dildo, then? It was awfully smooth for a dildo, though."

"There's more to cucumbers than salad, you know."

"Oh."

Hard Drives and Hard Bodies

Who says geeks can't have a love life? Look at Bill Gates. On second thought, he's a bad example—who wouldn't go out with a guy that has six-hundred gazillion dollars, even if he is the world's biggest pencil-neck and uglier than Alfred E. Newman to boot? (Pun intended—boot, as in boot up your computer. Get it?) Well, mount your floppies and connect your ribbon cable folks, 'cause you're about to read about—yes, it's unbelievable but true—a nerdy sex adventure.

Before you get completely turned off thinking this is going to be written in some super techno-nerd-speak, filled with computerese that you have as much chance of understanding as you do Swahili...well, you're partly correct. However, I promise to go easy on the technical stuff and go heavy on the hot stuff. I'll even throw in some translations when necessary. Later on there will be a pop quiz on terminology....

You have guessed by now that I'm the nerd-wannabe starring in this adventure. Correctamente. In my day job, I serve time at the local computer store manning the help desk. You know, I'm the one you call when you can't figure out why the sound card won't work, why the CD ROM drive won't work with the sound card, etc. I answer a myriad of questions ranging from the very basic (what's the "C" drive and what happens if I format it?) to giving out advice on networking (get your link between SNA and Ethernet established and your PCs will be able to hook up with your mainframes). Sounds real exciting, right? Are you hooked yet?

And for fun? What do I do at night? I get home, feed the animals (four cats and two dogs), zap a Healthy Choice in the microwave and go upstairs to my workroom where I either:

1) Finish rehabbing and/or building the computer one of my friends is paying me to work on;

2) Get on-line and download files I'll never have time to use, or maybe skip across the Internet and see what everyone else is up to;

3) Field calls from friends and relatives who want to pick my brain.

It's an exciting life, I know, and one everyone is dying to learn more about. Oh, I forgot weekends. Well, my weekends usually consist of either one or all of the three weeknight activities aforementioned, or if a computer show happens to be in town, I'll hop on over for some real adventure. Obviously, such a busy and thrilling life doesn't allow much time for romance...nor is romance very attracted to nerdiness.

My last relationship ended six months ago, and I guess I contributed greatly to its demise, according to Joyce. She said living with me was like living with a Maytag. I took that to mean that I was at least dependable, that you could always count on me and that I didn't need repairs. However, Joyce says that's not what she meant. I didn't get it. Maybe I'll never get it. And when Joyce moved out, she left me a very nice note saying she liked me and wished the best for me, but that it was hard living with someone who was as different from herself as I was—we were as far apart as night and day, she said. And then to put it in terms I'd relate to better, she said it was as if I were a Macintosh and she was an IBM. That I understood—two completely different operating systems.

She thanked me for building her a super-charged Pentium system, and said she'd leave the animals with me—something about they related better to me than her and vice-versa. After she left I just filled up my life even more with my integrated circuit friends, and now I don't really have time for a relationship. Or so I thought....

I do miss her, though. Maybe she has a point. I guess I could try and be more interested in things everybody else seems to like. Football, movies and women's golf. Last Saturday I planned on actually doing something different—going to a movie. I tried calling some of my friends from work but I couldn't interest any of them in seeing Stephen Hawking's *A Brief History of Time*. They all wanted to see *Mrs. Doubtfire*. They did invite me over to watch football the next day. I went and drank a couple of beers and watched, or tried to. I just couldn't get interested, and they were all so involved in the game. They knew the names of the players and their positions like they had known them all their lives. I did like the beer commercials, though. Especially the one with the Swedish Women's Massage Team. Why couldn't the game be more like the commercials?

I left at the halftime portion, saying something about feeding the animals. Maybe I'll never get it. As I left, I remembered there was a computer show at the Sheraton. Today was the last day. If you ever go to a computer show, never go the first day. Always wait until the last day and go late-like around two or three o'clock. Then you can get some deals, because most of the dealers don't want to cart all that inventory back on the truck. If you pay cash, you can really increase your haggling power.

One of my friends at the football party, Lou-Ann, had asked me about upgrading her 386 to a 486 processor (translation: it's like making a four cylinder engine into a six cylinder. More speed and power.) "Next time you're at a show, maybe you could pick one up for me," she said. Lou-Ann was kind of nice looking. Come to think of it, I wouldn't mind installing her upgrade, either… maybe there is hope after all. I decided to hit the ATM machine at the bank and high-tail it over to the show in search of last minute bargains on 486s.

On the way I stopped at a convenience store for some coffee. The beer had left me a little fuzzy-headed and I wanted to be sharp for some haggling. I made it to the hotel at three o'clock. Good timing. There was only an hour left until the show closed down. And it didn't look too crowded. Good. No lines and no fighting my way through a sea of people. Going to a computer show is akin to going to an electronic flea market. There are about five or six aisles and the dealers are lined up side by side, their tables laden with the wares of the day—monitors, CD ROM, hard drives, complete systems, etc. Used and new equipment, you name it, it's here. The biggest attractions are usually the complete systems displays and the adult CD inventory. I browsed the adult CDs and saw one that intrigued me—*Girls Doin' Girls*. Might be some nice entertainment tonight. I paid the twenty dollars and went off in search of motherboards.

Some of the dealers were actually packing it in for the day. What luck. These guys were really ready to deal, I bet. I stopped at one table and spied a young Asian man putting hard drives into styrofoam packing.

"Got any 486s?" I inquired.

He shrugged his shoulders and said, "Lee. Over here. Man wants 486."

This is not the first time I have been gender mistaken. My hair is pretty short and my attire is not what one would call overtly feminine—white T-shirt, baggy jeans, Doc Martens high tops, flannel shirt and a baseball cap with "Let's Do It In Groupware" splayed across the front. I didn't bother to correct him. He looked up from his packing and said, "My sister will help you," then continued his work.

I stared at the stacks of hard drives and was just about to ask him what his prices on one gig drives were, when a distinctly female voice said, "Can I help you?"

I looked up and opened my mouth but nothing came out. In front of me was a stunning Asian woman. She was a little shorter than I—she had to be about 5'2". Her long black hair was pulled back in a bun. She had a flannel shirt on, baggy jeans and work boots. Her face was indescribably beautiful. She was smiling. Maybe she was amused by the severity of my catatonic state, I don't know.

I tried again to get my mouth to work and amazingly something came out. "Motherboards," I stammered. "I'm looking for 486s. What do you have?"

She started laughing. I knew I must look like an idiot. "I am sorry. I must apologize for my brother. He called you a man. Tommy," she shouted, and then she said something in another language that sounded like a reprimand. I'm not sure. I didn't care. She could have been quoting the phone book for all I cared. Her voice sounded like bells. I felt like I was going to pass out. What was in that coffee? "You want 486s? We have them. SX or DX?" (translation: DX has a math-coprocessor, SX doesn't).

"DX, 25 megahertz (translation: speed). And 30-pin slots, please." I had seen Lou-Ann's 386 and knew she had 30-pin memory chips. It would be more economical to buy a 486 with 30-pin slots so we could re-use the chips.

The woman held up a processor board and said, "25 Megahertz, with 8 slots and the DX chip. $115."

Now $115 is a pretty good price and, had I been in the proper frame of mind, I would have tried to bargain it down to say $99. But I was completely unnerved by the beautiful creature in front of me and I blurted out, "I'll take it."

She said, "Are you building a new one or is this an upgrade?" I told her I was upgrading a 386 and she said, "What about the power supply?"

She was right. A 386 typically uses a smaller power supply, around 150 watts. The 486s and up require at least 200 watts. Lou-Ann would need a new power supply. I looked at the woman and said, "You're right. I'll need a power supply."

She pointed at the little rainbow pin on my shirt lapel and said, "Are you a member?" She then opened her flannel shirt to reveal a tee shirt that said I'M NOT GAY BUT MY GIRLFRIEND IS.

I said, "And who's your girlfriend?"

She shook her head and looked a little sad. "None. Had one. She wasn't into computers. How about you?" I started laughing and she said, "What's so funny?"

I then told her all about Joyce, about the Maytag comparison. I think I told her everything. All I know is I was still talking, she was laughing and then her brother came up and started screaming in that language again, pointing at his watch.

"It's almost 4 o'clock. We are almost packed up. I have a little mini-tower case with a 200 watt supply for $45. I'll give it to you with the 486 board for $125." Wow. That was a deal. A new case, power supply and motherboard for only $10 more than the board itself. I gave her the cash, she said, "Pull up around back where the loading docks are and I'll meet you with your stuff." I left the room, still feeling like I'd been hit by a truck. I had met another geek like myself. A gay geek. A beautiful gay geek. Wow.

I drove around the rear of the hotel to dock number three. She was there, sitting on the concrete landing next to my purchases, smiling. She helped me load it in the car and then I couldn't help it. I said, "Do you want to go somewhere and have coffee? I mean, we could continue our conversation. I think we have a lot in common."

She said, "I was thinking the same thing. My brother and I drove separately. He drove the truck and has to get back to New Jersey tonight, but I'm free for a while."

I don't know what made me do this, but suddenly I was possessed with a crazy thought. "You're going to think I'm crazy..."—she was still smiling at me—"...but I was thinking maybe we could, you know, get a room. Here at the hotel. We could just sit and talk, maybe get some room service." I was positive she would turn me down, but then she said, "Maybe not just talk." Her hand touched my arm and I felt a big bolt of lightning run down my arm. Sort of like a power surge, I guess. Then her hand moved up my arm and her fingers caressed my neck. Then she kissed me, right there on the loading dock. I closed my eyes and we stayed like that, just little kisses, gently tasting each other. I could feel my whole body tingling—something I knew I had felt somewhere in time. I was positive my circuits were gonna blow any second (translation: I was getting hot). "Lee, let's go get that room now," I breathed between kisses. She nodded her head; she was still kissing.

I drove us around to the front of the hotel. Her hands were all over me and I nearly hit one of the trucks, she made me swerve so violently. We went into the lobby, Lee walked over near the elevators and I obtained the key to Room 405. Paid cash, of course. I had enough cash left in my pocket to buy a super VGA color monitor (translation: $200). I walked over to Lee, we got in the elevator and we elevated to the fourth floor, the doors opened and we flew to the room. Barely inside the door, we picked up where we had left off. I placed my hands on her waist, tugging at her tee shirt until I had it out of her pants. Her hands moved up my shirt, landing on my breasts. My serial port speed jumped from 9600 bps to 28,800 (translation: my breathing was starting to get heavy and I felt major tingles now). Somehow we made it over to the bed and once there we proceeded to remove all articles of clothing and we slid under the covers. I lay on my back and she sat on top of me, strad-dling me. Her body was gorgeous—sleek, muscular, powerful. Like a 100 megahertz Pentium.

At this point, it is in the best interest of the story to completely abandon all references to computer parts and speak in plain English (translation: no more transla-tions—we're gettin' to the good stuff). It's hard for me, but I'm determined to do it.

I could feel her wetness between her legs as she straddled me, leaning over until her breasts were in my face. I sucked one breast, hearing her sigh with pleasure, and my hand moved up to play with the nipple on her other breast. I continued this action, back and forth between breasts. I could feel my own wetness start to trickle down my legs onto the sheets. She sat up, reached behind her head and undid her hair. It fell, cascading down across her shoulders. I touched it, feel-ing the silkiness and softness wash over my fingers like a cool breeze. And then she started to suck on my breasts while her hand played with my clit. Now the juice was really flowing, out of me, out of her. She slid farther down, her head between my legs and then I felt her tongue on my leg, gently tickling up my thigh. She did this to the other leg, then she thrust her tongue into my cunt and switched into overdrive (I don't think this needs a translation, do you?). I mean, she went into a higher gear. I was going onto a higher plane, that's for sure. Joyce and I had actually had sex at some point in our misunderstood togetherness, but I don't remember it being like this. Lee was literally eating me up, and I didn't want her to stop.

She said, "I want to fuck you. I want to make you come." Then she started. Her hand went inside and she was fucking me and sucking me. Then she said, "I wish I had my dildo."

I said, breathing rather heavily, "Don't worry about it. This is great."

But she got up and squealed, "I've got it!" For a moment I thought she really did carry a vibrator with her, for emergencies like this. I was convinced of that when she remounted me and I felt something hard and plastic slide into me. She moved the object in and out rhythmically, while she sucked my clit and twisted my nipple with the other hand. I just closed my eyes and rode the joyride of my life, trying to stay on the merry-go-round as long as I could. Finally all my circuits went kablooey and I came—one big, loud, exhausting scream, followed by little spasms and a torrent of wetness.

She lay on top of me, and when I had sufficiently recovered, I said, "Do you always carry a vibrator with you just in case?"

She turned her face up at me, smiling and said,

"That wasn't a vibrator. That was the battery from my laptop. I had it in my coat pocket—it's dead and I meant to replace it. I guess I won't now." She grinned and held up her hand. In her hand was the rather rectangular battery from an AST laptop. I was amazed. I didn't know batteries could be that useful once drained of all power. Suddenly the image of my workroom came to view, with a cardboard box filled with dead laptop batteries. I might have a little cottage industry on my hands.

"Could I borrow that?" I said. "I'd like to try a little experiment." She handed me the battery and said, "What do you mean?"

I started sucking on her breast, and between mouthfuls said, "If a dead battery can fuck two women in the same day, maybe it's not really dead after all."

She started laughing and said, "Okay, Mr. Gates. Start Me Up."

The Masquerade Erotic Newsletter

◆ ◆ ◆ ◆ ◆ ◆ ◆ ◆ ◆ ◆ ◆ ◆ ◆ ◆ ◆ ◆ ◆ ◆

FICTION, ESSAYS, REVIEWS, PHOTOGRAPHY, INTERVIEWS, EXPOSÉS, AND MUCH MORE!

"One of my favorite sex zines featuring some of the best articles on erotica, fetishes, sex clubs and the politics of porn." —*Factsheet Five*

"I recommend a subscription to *The Masquerade Erotic Newsletter....* They feature short articles on "the scene"...an occasional fiction piece, and reviews of other erotic literature. Recent issues have featured intelligent prose by the likes of Trish Thomas, David Aaron Clark, Pat Califia, Laura Antoniou, Lily Burana, John Preston, and others.... it's good stuff." —*Black Sheets*

"A classy, bi-monthly magazine..." —*Betty Paginated*

"It's always a treat to see a copy of *The Masquerade Erotic Newsletter,* for it brings a sophisticated and unexpected point of view to bear on the world of erotica, and does this with intelligence, tolerance, and compassion." —Martin Shepard, co-publisher, The Permanent Press

"Publishes great articles, interviews and pix which in many cases are truly erotic and which deal non-judgementally with the full array of human sexuality, a far cry from much of the material which passes itself off under that title.... *Masquerade Erotic Newsletter* is fucking great." —*Eddie, the Magazine*

"We always enjoy receiving your *Masquerade Newsletter* and seeing the variety of subjects covered...." —*body art*

"*Masquerade Erotic Newsletter* is probably the best newsletter I have ever seen." —*Secret International*

"The latest issue is absolutely lovely. Marvelous images...." —*The Boudoir Noir*

"I must say that the *Newsletter* is fabulous...."

—Tuppy Owens, Publisher, Author, Sex Therapist

"Fascinating articles on all aspects of sex..." —*Desire*

◆ ◆ ◆ ◆ ◆ ◆ ◆ ◆ ◆ ◆ ◆ ◆ ◆ ◆ ◆ ◆ ◆ ◆

ROSEBUD BOOKS

THE ROSEBUD READER

Rosebud Books—the hottest-selling line of lesbian erotica available—here collects the very best of the best. Rosebud has contributed greatly to the burgeoning genre of lesbian erotica—to the point that authors like Lindsay Welsh, Aarona Griffin and Valentina Cilescu are among the hottest and most closely watched names in lesbian and gay publishing. Here are the finest moments from Rosebud's contemporary classics. $5.95/319-8

K. T. BUTLER

TOOLS OF THE TRADE

A sparkling mix of lesbian erotica and humor. A sizzling encounter with ice cream, cappucino and chocolate cake; an affair with a complete stranger; a pair of faulty handcuffs and love on a drafting table. Seventeen delightful tales.
$5.95/420-8

LOVECHILD

GAG

From New York's thriving poetry scene comes this explosive volume of work from one of the bravest, most cutting young writers you'll ever encounter. The poems in *Gag* take on American hypocrisy with uncommon energy, and announce Lovechild as a writer of unique and unforgettable rage. $5.95/369-4

ALISON TYLER

THE VIRGIN

Does he satisfy you? Is something missing? Maybe you don't need a man at all—maybe you need me. Veronica answers a personal ad in the "Women Seeking Women" category—and discovers a whole sensual world she never knew existed! And she never dreamed she'd be prized as a virgin all over again, by someone who would deflower her with a passion no man could ever show.... $5.95/379-1

THE BLUE ROSE

The tale of a modern sorority—fashioned after a Victorian girls' school. Ignited to the heights of passion by erotic tales of the Victorian age, a group of lusty young women are encouraged to act out their forbidden fantasies—all under the tutelage of Mistresses Emily and Justine, two avid practitioners of hard-core discipline! $5.95/335-X

ELIZABETH OLIVER

THE SM MURDER: Murder at Roman Hill

Intrepid lesbian P.I.s Leslie Patrick and Robin Penny take on a really hot case: the murder of the notorious Felicia Roman. The circumstances of the crime lead the pair on an excursion through the leatherdyke underground, where motives—and desires—run deep. But as Leslie and Robin soon find, every woman harbors her own closely guarded secret.... $5.95/353-8

PAGAN DREAMS

Cassidy and Samantha plan a vacation at a secluded bed-and-breakfast, hoping for a little personal time alone. Their hostess, however, has different plans. The lovers are plunged into a world of dungeons and pagan rites, as the merciless Anastasia steals Samantha for her own. B&B—B&D-style! $5.95/295-7

SUSAN ANDERS

CITY OF WOMEN

A collection of stories dedicated to women and the passions that draw them together. Designed strictly for the sensual pleasure of women, Anders' tales are set to ignite flames of passion from coast to coast. The residents of *City of Women* hold the key to even the most forbidden fantasies. $5.95/375-9

ROSEBUD BOOKS

PINK CHAMPAGNE

Tasty, torrid tales of butch/femme couplings—from a writer more than capable of describing the special fire ignited when opposites collide. Tough as nails or soft as silk, these women seek out their antitheses, intent on working out the details of their own personal theory of difference. $5.95/282-5

LAVENDER ROSE

Anonymous

A classic collection of lesbian literature: From the writings of Sappho, Queen of the island Lesbos, to the turn-of-the-century *Black Book of Lesbianism*; from *Tips to Maidens* to *Crimson Hairs*, a recent lesbian saga—here are the great but little-known lesbian writings and revelations. $4.95/208-6

EDITED BY LAURA ANTONIOU

LEATHERWOMEN II

A follow-up volume to the popular and controversial *Leatherwomen*. Laura Antoniou turns an editor's discerning eye to the writing of women on the edge—resulting in a collection sure to ignite libidinal flames. Leave taboos behind—because these Leatherwomen know no limits.... $4.95/229-9

LEATHERWOMEN

These fantasies, from the pens of new or emerging authors, break every rule imposed on women's fantasies. The hottest stories from some of today's newest and most outrageous writers make this an unforgettable exploration of the female libido. $4.95/3095-4

LESLIE CAMERON

THE WHISPER OF FANS

"Just looking into her eyes, she felt that she knew a lot about this woman. She could see strength, boldness, a fresh sense of aliveness that rocked her to the core. In turn she felt open, revealed under the woman's gaze—all her secrets already told. No need of shame or artifice...." $5.95/259-0

AARONA GRIFFIN

PASSAGE AND OTHER STORIES

An S/M romance. Lovely Nina is frightened by her lesbian passions until she finds herself infatuated with a woman she spots at a local café. One night Nina follows her and finds herself enmeshed in an endless maze leading to a world where women test the edges of sexuality and power. $4.95/3057-1

VALENTINA CILESCU

THE ROSEBUD SUTRA

"Women are hardly ever known in their true light, though they may love others, or become indifferent towards them, may give them delight, or abandon them, or may extract from them all the wealth that they possess." So says *The Rosebud Sutra*—a volume promising women's inner secrets. One woman learns to use these secrets in a quest for pleasure with a succession of lady loves.... $4.95/242-6

THE HAVEN

J craves domination, and her perverse appetites lead her to the Haven: the isolated sanctuary Ros and Annie call home. Soon J forces her way into the couple's world, bringing unspeakable lust and cruelty into their lives. $4.95/165-9

MISTRESS MINE

Sophia Cranleigh sits in prison, accused of authoring the "obscene" *Mistress Mine*. For Sophia has led no ordinary life, but has slaved and suffered—deliciously—under the hand of the notorious Mistress Malin. How long had she languished under the dominance of this incredible beauty? $5.95/445-3

ROSEBUD BOOKS

LINDSAY WELSH

MILITARY SECRETS

Colonel Candice Sproule heads a highly-specialized boot camp. Assisted by three dominatrix sergeants, Col. Sproule takes on the talented submissives sent to her by secret military contacts. Then comes Jesse Robbins —whose pleasure in being served matches the Colonel's own. This new recruit sets off fireworks in the barracks—and beyond—and soon earns the respect of even her stern Commander.... $5.95/397-X

ROMANTIC ENCOUNTERS

Beautiful Julie, the most powerful editor of romance novels in the industry, spends her days igniting women's passions through books—and her nights fulfilling those needs with a variety of lovers. Julie's two worlds come together with the type of bodice-ripping Harlequin could never imagine! $5.95/359-7

THE BEST OF LINDSAY WELSH

A collection of this popular writer's best work. This author was one of Rosebud's early bestsellers, and remains highly popular. A sampler set to introduce some of the hottest lesbian erotica to a wider audience. $5.95/368-6

PROVINCETOWN SUMMER

This completely original collection is devoted exclusively to white-hot desire between women. From the casual encounters of women on the prowl to the enduring erotic bonds between old lovers, the women of *Provincetown Summer* will set your senses on fire! A national bestseller. $5.95/362-7

NECESSARY EVIL

What's a girl to do? When her Mistress proves too systematic, too by-the-book, one lovely submissive takes the ultimate chance—choosing and creating a Mistress who'll fulfill her heart's desire. Little did she know how difficult it would be—and, in the end, rewarding.... $5.95/277-9

A VICTORIAN ROMANCE

Lust-letters from the road. A young Englishwoman realizes her dream—a trip abroad under the guidance of her eccentric maiden aunt. Soon the young but blossoming Elaine comes to discover her own sexual talents, as a hot-blooded Parisian named Madelaine takes her Sapphic education in hand. Another Welsh winner! $5.95/365-1

A CIRCLE OF FRIENDS

The author of the nationally best-selling *Provincetown Summer* returns with the story of a remarkable group of women. Slowly, the women pair off to explore all the possibilities of lesbian passion, until finally it seems that there is nothing—and no one—they have not dabbled in. A stunning tribute to truly special relationships. $4.95/250-7

PRIVATE LESSONS

A high voltage tale of life at The Whitfield Academy for Young Women— where cruel headmistress Devon Whitfield presides over the in-depth education of only the most talented and delicious of maidens! Elizabeth Dunn arrives at the Academy, where it becomes clear that she has much to learn—to the delight of Devon Whitfield and her randy staff of Mistresses! Another contemporary classic from Lindsay Welsh. $4.95/116-0

BAD HABITS

What does one do with a poorly trained slave? Break her of her bad habits, of course! The story of the ultimate finishing school, *Bad Habits* was an immediate favorite with women nationwide. "Talk about passing the wet test!... If you like hot, lesbian erotica, run—don't walk...and pick up a copy of *Bad Habits.*"—*Lambda Book Report* $5.95/446-1

ROSEBUD BOOKS

ANNABELLE BARKER

MOROCCO

A luscious young woman stands to inherit a fortune—if she can only withstand the ministrations of her cruel guardian until her twentieth birthday. With two months left, Lila makes a bold bid for freedom, only to find that liberty has its own excruciating and delicious price.... $4.95/148-9

A.L. REINE

DISTANT LOVE & OTHER STORIES

A book of seductive tales. In the title story, Leah Michaels and her lover Ranelle have had four years of blissful, smoldering passion together. One night, when Ranelle is out of town, Leah records an audio "Valentine," a cassette filled with erotic reminiscences.... $4.95/3056-3

RHINOCEROS BOOKS

EDITED BY THOMAS S. ROCHE

NOIROTICA: An Anthology of Erotic Crime Stories

A collection of darkly sexy tales, taking place at the crossroads of the crime and erotic genres. Thomas Roche has gathered together some of today's finest writers of sexual fiction, all of whom explore the murky terrain where desire runs irrevocably afoul of the law. Carol Queen, Bill Brent, Simon Sheppard, Cecilia Tan, Amelia G., M. Christian and many others are represented by their most hard-bitten, hard-hitting tales. $6.95/390-2

DAVID MELTZER

UNDER

Under is the story of a sex professional, whose life at the bottom of the social heap is, nevertheless, filled with incident. Other than numerous surgeries designed to increase his physical allure, he is faced with an establishment intent on using any body for genetic experiments. These forces drive the cyber-gigolo underground—where even more bizarre cultures await.... $6.95/290-6

ORF

He is the ultimate musician-hero—the idol of thousands, the fevered dream of many more. And like many musicians before him, he is misunderstood, misused—and totally out of control. Every last drop of feeling is squeezed from a modern-day troubadour and his lady love. $6.95/110-1

EDITED BY AMARANTHA KNIGHT

FLESH FANTASTIC

Humans have long toyed with the idea of "playing God": creating life from nothingness, bringing Life to the inanimate. Now Amarantha Knight, author of the "Darker Passions" series of erotic horror novels, collects stories exploring not only the allure of Creation, but the lust that follows.... $6.95/352-X

GARY BOWEN

DIARY OF A VAMPIRE

"Gifted with a darkly sensual vision and a fresh voice, [Bowen] is a writer to watch out for."   —Cecilia Tan

The chilling, arousing, and ultimately moving memoirs of an undead—but all too human—soul. Bowen's Rafael, a red-blooded male with an insatiable hunger for same, is the perfect antidote to the effete malcontents haunting bookstores today. *Diary of a Vampire* marks the emergence of a bold and brilliant vision, firmly rooted in past *and* present. $6.95/331-7

RHINOCEROS BOOKS

RENÉ MAIZEROY

FLESHLY ATTRACTIONS

Lucien Hardanges was the son of the wantonly beautiful actress, Marie-Rose Hardanges. When she decides to let a "friend" introduce her son to the pleasures of love, Marie-Rose could not have foretold the erotic excesses that would lead to her own ruin and that of her cherished son. $6.95/299-X

EDITED BY LAURA ANTONIOU

NO OTHER TRIBUTE

A collection of stories sure to challenge Political Correctness in a way few have before, with tales of women kept in bondage to their lovers by their deepest passions. Love pushes these women beyond acceptable limits, rendering them helpless to deny the men and women they adore. $6.95/294-9

SOME WOMEN

Over forty essays written by women actively involved in consensual dominance and submission. Professional mistresses, lifestyle leatherdykes, whipmakers, titleholders—women from every conceivable walk of life lay bare their true feelings about about issues as explosive as feminism, abuse, pleasures and public image. $6.95/300-7

BY HER SUBDUED

Stories of women who get what they want. The tales in this collection all involve women in control—of their lives, their loves, their men. So much in control, in fact, that they can remorselessly break rules to become the powerful goddesses of the men who sacrifice all to worship at their feet. Woman Power with a vengeance! $6.95/281-7

JEAN STINE

SEASON OF THE WITCH

"A future in which it is technically possible to transfer the total mind... of a rapist killer into the brain dead but physically living body of his female victim. Remarkable for intense psychological technique. There is eroticism but it is necessary to mark the differences between the sexes and the subtle altering of a man into a woman." —*The Science Fiction Critic* $6.95/268-X

JOHN WARREN

THE TORQUEMADA KILLER

Detective Eva Hernandez has finally gotten her first "big case": a string of vicious murders taking place within New York's SM community. Piece by piece, Eva assembles the evidence, revealing a picture of a world misunderstood and under attack—and gradually comes to understand her own place within it. A hot, edge-of-the-seat thriller from the author of *The Loving Dominant*—and an exciting insider's perspective on "the scene." $6.95/367-8

THE LOVING DOMINANT

Everything you need to know about an infamous sexual variation—and an unspoken type of love. Mentor—a longtime player in the dominance/submission scene—guides readers through this world and reveals the too-often hidden basis of the D/S relationship: care, trust and love. $6.95/218-3

GRANT ANTREWS

SUBMISSIONS

Once again, Antrews portrays the very special elements of the dominant/submissive relationship...with restraint—this time with the story of a lonely man, a winning lottery ticket, and a demanding dominatrix. One of erotica's most discerning writers. $6.95/207-8

RHINOCEROS BOOKS

MY DARLING DOMINATRIX

When a man and a woman fall in love it's supposed to be simple, uncomplicated, easy—unless that woman happens to be a dominatrix. Curiosity gives way to unblushing desire in this story of one man's awakening to the joys to be experienced as the willing slave of a powerful woman. A perennial favorite
$6.95/447-X

LAURA ANTONIOU WRITING AS "SARA ADAMSON"

THE TRAINER

The long-awaited conclusion of Adamson's stunning Marketplace Trilogy! The ultimate underground sexual realm includes not only willing slaves, but the exquisite trainers who take submissives firmly in hand. And it is now the time for these mentors to divulge their own secrets—the desires that led them to become the ultimate figures of authority. $6.95/249-3

THE SLAVE

The second volume in the "Marketplace" trilogy. *The Slave* covers the experience of one exceptionally talented submissive who longs to join the ranks of those who have proven themselves worthy of entry into the Marketplace. But the price, while delicious, is staggeringly high.... Adamson's plot thickens, as her trilogy moves to a conclusion in *The Trainer*. $6.95/173-X

THE MARKETPLACE

"Merchandise does not come easily to the Marketplace.... They haunt the clubs and the organizations.... Some are so ripe that they intimidate the poseurs, the weekend sadists and the furtive dilettantes who are so endemic to that world. And they never stop asking where we may be found...." $6.95/3096-2

THE CATALYST

After viewing a controversial, explicitly kinky film full of images of bondage and submission, several audience members find themselves deeply moved by the erotic suggestions they've seen on the screen. "Sara Adamson"'s sensational debut volume! $5.95/328-7

DAVID AARON CLARK

SISTER RADIANCE

A chronicle of obsession, rife with Clark's trademark vivisections of contemporary desires, sacred and profane. The vicissitudes of lust and romance are examined against a backdrop of urban decay and shallow fashionability in this testament to the allure—and inevitability—of the forbidden. $6.95/215-9

THE WET FOREVER

The story of Janus and Madchen, a small-time hood and a beautiful sex worker, *The Wet Forever* examines themes of loyalty, sacrifice, redemption and obsession amidst Manhattan's sex parlors and underground S/M clubs. Its combination of sex and suspense led Terence Sellers to proclaim it "evocative and poetic." $6.95/117-9

ALICE JOANOU

BLACK TONGUE

"Joanou has created a series of sumptuous, brooding, dark visions of sexual obsession and is undoubtedly a name to look out for in the future."
—*Redeemer*

Another seductive book of dreams from the author of the acclaimed *Tourniquet*. Exploring lust at its most florid and unsparing, *Black Tongue* is a trove of baroque fantasies—each redolent of the forbidden. Joanou creates some of erotica's most mesmerizing and unforgettable characters. $6.95/258-2

RHINOCEROS BOOKS

TOURNIQUET

A heady collection of stories and effusions from the pen of one our most dazzling young writers. Strange tales abound, from the story of the mysterious and cruel Cybele, to an encounter with the sadistic entertainment of a bizarre after-hours cafe. A sumptuous feast for all the senses. $6.95/3060-1

CANNIBAL FLOWER

"She is waiting in her darkened bedroom, as she has waited throughout history, to seduce the men who are foolish enough to be blinded by her irresistible charms....She is the goddess of sexuality, and *Cannibal Flower* is her haunting siren song."—Michael Perkins $4.95/72-6

MICHAEL PERKINS

EVIL COMPANIONS

Set in New York City during the tumultuous waning years of the Sixties, *Evil Companions* has been hailed as "a frightening classic." A young couple explores the nether reaches of the erotic unconscious in a shocking confrontation with the extremes of passion. With a new introduction by science fiction legend Samuel R. Delany. $6.95/3067-9

AN ANTHOLOGY OF CLASSIC ANONYMOUS EROTIC WRITING

Michael Perkins, acclaimed authority on erotic literature, has collected the very best passages from the world's erotic writing—especially for Rhino*ceros* readers. "Anonymous" is one of the most infamous bylines in publishing history—and these steamy excerpts show why! $6.95/140-3

THE SECRET RECORD: Modern Erotic Literature

Michael Perkins surveys the field with authority and unique insight. Updated and revised to include the latest trends, tastes, and developments in this misunderstood and maligned genre. $6.95/3039-3

HELEN HENLEY

ENTER WITH TRUMPETS

Helen Henley was told that woman just don't write about sex—much less the taboos she was so interested in exploring. So Henley did it alone, flying in the face of "tradition" by producing *Enter With Trumpets*, a touching tale of arousal and devotion in one couple's kinky relationship. $6.95/197-7

PHILIP JOSE FARMER

FLESH

Space Commander Stagg explored the galaxies for 800 years. Upon his return, the hero Stagg is made the centerpiece of an incredible public ritual—one that will repeatedly take him to the heights of ecstasy, and inexorably drag him toward the depths of hell. $6.95/303-1

A FEAST UNKNOWN

"Sprawling, brawling, shocking, suspenseful, hilarious..."

—Theodore Sturgeon

Farmer's supreme anti-hero returns. "I was conceived and born in 1888." Slowly, Lord Grandrith—armed with the belief that he is the son of Jack the Ripper—tells the story of his remarkable and unbridled life. His story begins with his discovery of the secret of immortality.... $6.95/276-0

THE IMAGE OF THE BEAST

Herald Childe has seen Hell, glimpsed its horror in an act of sexual mutilation. Childe must now find and destroy an inhuman predator through the streets of a polluted and decadent Los Angeles of the future. One clue after another leads Childe to an inescapable realization about the nature of sex and evil.... $6.95/166-7

RHINOCEROS BOOKS

LEOPOLD VON SACHER-MASOCH

VENUS IN FURS

This classic 19th century novel is the first uncompromising exploration of the dominant/submissive relationship in literature. The alliance of Severin and Wanda epitomizes Sacher-Masoch's dark obsession with a cruel, controlling goddess and the urges that drive the man held in her thrall. Includes the letters exchanged between Sacher-Masoch and Emilie Mataja—an aspiring writer he sought as the avatar of his forbidden desires. $6.95/3089-X

SAMUEL R. DELANY

THE MAD MAN

"The latest novel from Hugo- and Nebula-winning science fiction writer and critic Delany...reads like a pornographic reflection of Peter Ackroyd's *Chatterton* or A. S. Byatt's *Possession*.... The pornographic element... becomes more than simple shock or titillation, though, as Delany develops an insightful dichotomy between [his protagonist]'s two worlds: the one of cerebral philosophy and dry academia, the other of heedless, 'impersonal' obsessive sexual extremism. When these worlds finally collide...the novel achieves a surprisingly satisfying resolution...."   —*Publishers Weekly*

Science fiction legend Samuel R. Delany's most provocative novel. For his thesis, graduate student John Marr researches the life and work of the brilliant Timothy Hasler: a philosopher whose career was cut tragically short over a decade earlier. On another front, Marr finds himself increasingly drawn toward more shocking, depraved sexual entanglements with the homeless men of his neighborhood, until it begins to seem that Hasler's death might hold some key to his own life as a gay man in the age of AIDS. $8.99/408-9/mass market

EQUINOX

The *Scorpion* has sailed the seas in a quest for every possible pleasure. Her crew is a collection of the young, the twisted, the insatiable. A drifter comes into their midst, and is taken on a fantastic journey to the darkest, most dangerous sexual extremes—until he is finally a victim to their boundless appetites. $6.95/157-8

DANIEL VIAN

ILLUSIONS

Two tales of danger and desire in Berlin on the eve of WWII. From private homes to lurid cafés, passion is exposed and explored in stark contrast to the brutal violence of the time. A singularly arousing volume. $6.95/3074-1

PERSUASIONS

"The stockings are drawn tight by the suspender belt, tight enough to be stretched to the limit just above the middle part of her thighs..." A double novel, including the classics *Adagio* and *Gabriela and the General*, this volume traces desire around the globe. International lust! $6.95/183-7

ANDREI CODRESCU

THE REPENTANCE OF LORRAINE

"One of our most prodigiously talented and magical writers."

                                        —*NYT Book Review*

By the acclaimed author of *The Hole in the Flag* and *The Blood Countess*. An aspiring writer, a professor's wife, a secretary, gold anklets, Maoists, Roman harlots—and more—swirl through this spicy tale of a harried quest for a mythic artifact. Written when the author was a young man, this lusty yarn was inspired by the heady days of the Sixties. Includes a new Introduction by the author, painting a portrait of *Lorraine*'s creation. $6.95/329-5

RHINOCEROS BOOKS

SOPHIE GALLEYMORE BIRD
MANEATER

Through a bizarre act of creation, a man attains the "perfect" lover—by all appearances a beautiful, sensuous woman but in reality something far darker. Once brought to life she will accept no mate, seeking instead the prey that will sate her hunger for vengeance. A biting take on the war of the sexes, this debut goes for the jugular of the "perfect woman" myth. $6.95/103-9

TUPPY OWENS
SENSATIONS

A piece of porn history. Tuppy Owens tells the unexpurgated story of the making of *Sensations*—the first big-budget sex flick. Originally commissioned to appear in book form after the release of the film in 1975, *Sensations* is finally released under Masquerade's stylish Rhino*ceros* imprint. $6.95/3081-4

LIESEL KULIG
LOVE IN WARTIME

An uncompromising look at the politics, perils and pleasures of sexual power. Madeleine knew that the handsome SS officer was a dangerous man. But she was just a cabaret singer in Nazi-occupied Paris, trying to survive in a perilous time. When Josef fell in love with her, he discovered that a beautiful and amoral woman can sometimes be wildly dangerous. $6.95/3044-X

MASQUERADE BOOKS

TABITHA'S TEASE *Robin Wilde*
The Valentine Academy: an ultra-exclusive, all-girl institution, soon to receive its first male charge. When poor Robin arrives, he finds himself subject to the tortuous teasing of Tabitha—the Academy's most notoriously domineering co-ed. What Robin doesn't realize—but soon learns—is that Tabitha is pledge-mistress of a secret sorority dedicated to enslaving young men. Soon he finds himself a captive of Tabitha & Company's weird desires! $5.95/387-2

HELLFIRE *Charles G. Wood*
A vicious murderer is running amok in New York's sexual underground—and Nick O'Shay, a virile detective with the NYPD, plunges deep into the case. He soon becomes embroiled in an elusive world of fleshly extremes, hunting a madman seeking to purge America with fire and blood sacrifices.
"[Wood] betrays a photographer's eye for tableau and telling detail in his evocation of the larger-than-life figures of the late-'70s to mid-'80s sexual demimonde." —David Aaron Clark, author of *The Wet Forever*
$5.95/358-9

PIRATE'S SLAVE *Erica Bronte*
Lovely young Erica is stranded in a country where lust knows no bounds. Desperate to escape, she finds herself trading her firm, luscious body to any and all men willing and able to help her. Her adventure has its ups and downs, ins and outs—all to the undeniable pleasure of lusty Erica! $5.95/376-7

THE MISTRESS OF CASTLE ROHMENSTADT
Olivia M. Ravensworth
Lovely Katherine inherits a secluded European castle from a mysterious relative. Upon arrival, she discovers, much to her delight, that the castle is a haven of sensual pleasure. Katherine learns to shed her inhibitions and enjoy her new home's many delights. $5.95/372-4

TENDER BUNS *P. N. Dedeaux*
Meet Marc Merlin, the wizard of discipline! In a fashionable Canadian suburb, Merlin indulges his yen for punishment with an assortment of the town's most desirable and willing women. Things come to a rousing climax at a party planned to cater to just those whims Marc is most able to satisfy.... $5.95/396-1

COMPLIANCE *N. Whallen*
Fourteen stories exploring the pleasures of release. Characters from many walks of life learn to trust in the skills of others, only to experience the thrilling liberation of submission. Here are the real joys to be found in some of the most forbidden sexual practices around.... $5.95/356-2

LA DOMME: A DOMINATRIX ANTHOLOGY *Edited by Claire Baeder*
A steamy smorgasbord of female domination! Erotic literature has long been filled with heartstopping portraits of domineering women, and now the most memorable come together in one beautifully brutal volume. $5.95/366-X

THE GEEK *Tiny Alice*
"An adventure novel told by a sex-bent male mini-pygmy. This is an accomplishment of which anybody may be proud."—Philip José Farmer
The Geek is told from the point of view of, well, a chicken who reports on the various perversities he witnesses as part of a traveling carnival. When a gang of renegade lesbians kidnaps Chicken and his geek, all hell breaks loose. A strange tale, filled with outrageous erotic oddities. $5.95/341-4

SEX ON THE NET *Charisse van der Lyn*
Electrifying erotica from one of the Internet's hottest and most widely read authors. Encounters of all kinds—straight, lesbian, dominant/submissive and all sorts of extreme passions—are explored in thrilling detail. Discover what's turning on hackers from coast to coast! $5.95/399-6

MASQUERADE BOOKS

BEAUTY OF THE BEAST   *Carole Remy*
A shocking tell-all, written from the point-of-view of a prize-winning reporter.
And what reporting she does! All the secrets of an uninhibited life are
revealed, and each lusty tableau is painted in glowing colors. Join in on her
scandalous adventures—and reap the rewards of her extensive background in
Erotic Affairs! $5.95/332-5

NAUGHTY MESSAGE   *Stanley Carten*
Wesley Arthur, a withdrawn computer engineer, discovers a lascivious message on his answering machine. Aroused beyond his wildest dreams by the
unmentionable acts described, Wesley becomes obsessed with tracking down
the woman behind the seductive voice. His search takes him through strip
clubs and no-tell motels—and finally to his randy reward.... $5.95/333-3

The Marquis de Sade's JULIETTE   *David Aaron Clark*
The Marquis de Sade's infamous Juliette returns—and at the hand of David
Aaron Clark, she emerges as the most powerful, perverse and destructive
nightstalker modern New York will ever know. Under this domina's tutelage,
two women come to know torture's bizarre attractions, as they grapple with
the price of Juliette's promise of immortality.
Praise for Dave Clark:
**"David Aaron Clark has delved into one of the most sensationalistically
taboo aspects of eros, sadomasochism, and produced a novel of unmistak-
able literary imagination and artistic value."   —Carlo McCormick, *Paper***
                                                            $5.95/240-X

THE PARLOR   *N.T. Morley*
Lovely Kathryn gives in to the ultimate temptation. The mysterious John and
Sarah ask her to be their slave—an idea that turns Kathryn on so much that
she can't refuse! But who are these two mysterious strangers? Little by little,
Kathryn comes to know the inner secrets of her stunning keepers.$5.95/291-4

NADIA   *Anonymous*
"Nadia married General the Count Gregorio Stenoff—a gentleman of noble
pedigree it is true, but one of the most reckless dissipated rascals in Russia..."
Follow the delicious but neglected Nadia as she works to wring every drop of
pleasure out of life—despite an unhappy marriage. A classic title providing a
peek into the secret sexual lives of another time and place. $5.95/267-1

THE STORY OF A VICTORIAN MAID   *Nigel McParr*
What were the Victorians really like? Chances are, no one believes they were
as stuffy as their Queen, but who would have imagined such unbridled lib-
ertines! One maid is followed from exploit to smutty exploit, and all secrets
are revealed! $5.95/241-8

CARRIE'S STORY   *Molly Weatherfield*
"I had been Jonathan's slave for about a year when he told me he wanted to
sell me at an auction. I wasn't in any condition to respond when he told me
this..." Desire and depravity run rampant in this story of uncompromising
mastery and irrevocable submission. $5.95/444-5

CHARLY'S GAME   *Bren Flemming*
A rich woman's gullible daughter has run off with one of the toughest leather
dykes in town—and sexy P.I. Charly's hired to lure the girl back. One by one,
wise and wicked women ensnare one another in their lusty nets! $4.95/221-3

ANDREA AT THE CENTER   *J.P. Kansas*
Lithe and lovely young Andrea is, without warning, whisked away to a distant
retreat. There she is introduced to the ways of the Center, and soon becomes
quite friendly with its other inhabitants—all of whom are learning to abandon
restraint in their pursuit of the deepest sexual satisfaction. $5.95/324-4

MASQUERADE BOOKS

ASK ISADORA
Isadora Alman

An essential volume, collecting six years' worth of Isadora Alman's syndicated columns on sex and relationships. Alman's been called a "hip Dr. Ruth," and a "sexy Dear Abby," based upon the wit and pertinence of her advice. Today's world is more perplexing than ever—and Isadora Alman is just the expert to help untangle the most personal of knots.
$4.95/61-0

THE SLAVES OF SHOANNA
Mercedes Kelly

Shoanna, the cruel and magnificent, takes four maidens under her wing—and teaches them the ins and outs of pleasure and discipline. Trained in every imaginable perversion, from simple fleshly joys to advanced techniques, these students go to the head of the class!
$4.95/164-0

LOVE & SURRENDER
Marlene Darcy

"Madeline saw Harry looking at her legs and she blushed as she remembered what he wanted to do.... She casually pulled the skirt of her dress back to uncover her knees and the lower part of her thighs.... She tugged at her skirt again, pulled it back far enough so almost all of her thighs were exposed...."
$4.95/3082-2

THE COMPLETE *PLAYGIRL* FANTASIES
Editors of Playgirl

The best women's fantasies are collected here, fresh from the pages of *Playgirl*. These knockouts from the infamous "Reader's Fantasy Forum" prove, once again, that truth can indeed be hotter, wilder, and *better* than fiction.
$4.95/3075-X

STASI SLUT
Anthony Bobarzynski

Need we say more? Adina lives in East Germany, far from the sexually liberated, uninhibited debauchery of the West. She meets a group of ruthless and corrupt STASI agents who use her as a pawn in their political chess game as well as for their own perverse gratification—until she uses her talents and attractions in a final bid for total freedom!
$4.95/3050-4

BLUE TANGO
Hilary Manning

Ripe and tempting Julie is haunted by the sounds of extraordinary passion beyond her bedroom wall. Alone, she fantasizes about taking part in the amorous dramas of her hosts, Claire and Edward. When she finds a way to watch the nightly debauch, her curiosity turns to full-blown lust—and soon Julie's eager to join in!
$4.95/3037-7

LOUISE BELHAVEL

FRAGRANT ABUSES

The saga of Clara and Iris continues as the now-experienced girls enjoy themselves with a new circle of worldly friends whose imaginations match their own. Perversity follows the lusty ladies around the globe!
$4.95/88-2

DEPRAVED ANGELS

The final installment in the incredible adventures of Clara and Iris. Together with their friends, lovers, and worldly acquaintances, Clara and Iris explore the frontiers of depravity at home and abroad.
$4.95/92-0

TITIAN BERESFORD

THE WICKED HAND

With a special Introduction by *Leg Show*'s Dian Hanson. A collection of fanciful fetishistic tales featuring the absolute subjugation of men by lovely, domineering women. From Japan and Germany to the American heartland—these stories uncover the other side of the "weaker sex."
$5.95/343-0

CINDERELLA

Beresford triumphs again with this intoxicating tale, filled with castle dungeons and tightly corseted ladies-in-waiting, naughty viscounts and impossibly cruel masturbatrixes—nearly every conceivable method of erotic torture is explored and described in lush, vivid detail.
$4.95/305-8

MASQUERADE BOOKS

JUDITH BOSTON
Young Edward would have been lucky to get the stodgy old companion he thought his parents had hired for him. Instead, an exquisite woman arrives at his door, and Edward finds his compulsively lewd behavior never goes unpunished by the unflinchingly severe Judith Boston! $4.95/273-6

NINA FOXTON
An aristocrat finds herself bored by run-of-the-mill amusements for "ladies of good breeding." Instead of taking tea with proper gentlemen, naughty Nina invents a contraption to "milk" them of their most private essences. No man ever says "No" to Nina! $5.95/443-7

A TITIAN BERESFORD READER
Wild dominatrixes, perverse masochists, and mesmerizing detail are the hallmarks of the Beresford tale—and encountered here in abundance. The very best scenarios from all of Beresford's bestsellers make this a must-have for the Compleat Fetishist. $4.95/114-4

CHINA BLUE
KUNG FU NUNS
"When I could stand the pleasure no longer, she lifted me out of the chair and sat me down on top of the table. She then lifted her skirt. The sight of her perfect legs clad in white stockings and a petite garter belt further mesmerized me. I lean particularly towards white garter belts." China Blue returns! $4.95/3031-8

HARRIET DAIMLER
DARLING • INNOCENCE
In *Darling*, a virgin is raped by a mugger. Driven by her urge for revenge, she searches New York in a furious sexual hunt that leads to rape and murder. In *Innocence*, a young invalid determines to experience sex through her voluptuous nurse. Two critically acclaimed novels. $4.95/3047-4

LYN DAVENPORT
DOVER ISLAND
Off the coast of Oregon, Dr. David Kelly has planted the seeds of his dream—a Corporal Punishment Resort. Soon, many people from varied walks of life descend upon this isolated retreat, intent on fulfilling their every desire. Included in this elite gathering is Marcy Harris, who will prove the perfect partner for the lonely but lustful Doctor.... $5.95/384-8

TESSA'S HOLIDAYS
Tessa Duncan dreads the thought of another long winter in her small, drab Midwestern town—particularly after a summer filled with the intrigue and erotic surprise provided by her voracious lover, Grant. Soon however, Tessa learns that she needn't fear being bored—not with lusty Grant on the job! He soon makes sure that each of Tessa's holidays is filled with the type of sensual adventure most young women only dream about. What will her insatiable man dream up next? Only he knows—and he keeps his secrets until the lovely Tessa is ready to explode with desire! $5.95/377-5

THE GUARDIAN
Felicia grew up under the tutelage of the lash—and she learned her lessons well. Sir Rodney Wentworth has long searched for a woman capable of fulfilling his cruel desires, and after learning of Felicia's talents, sends for her. Upon arrival in his home, Felicia discovers that the "position" offered her is delightfully different than anything she could have expected! $5.95/371-6